'We're not here   ' said Hermione. 'This v   d hall, then left down a   which Mitten opened wi   did so, irritating Dr Frint   ys and locks were so old and primitive as to be quite po̶̶s̶s̶.̶ Any eight-year-old with a piece of stiff card and a modicum of ingenuity could have broken in without the slightest problem. Bognor was about to protest that he personally found lock-picking an extraordinarily difficult art to master when the door did finally open and Hermione let out an ungrammatical sentence composed entirely of expletives which Bognor found surprisingly strong, even for her.

'Someone else had the same idea,' said Bognor, following her into the room and eyeing the open filing cabinets and scattered papers. The burglar had been messy.

'What makes you say that?' asked Mitten, gaping at the papers. He looked both perplexed and outraged. This was more than an ordinary burglary, it was an affront to the college. That was what his manner suggested.

'Simon's right,' said Hermione. She bent down and scooped up a sheaf. 'Putney, Earl of,' she intoned. 'Unpromising material but enough means to compensate. Gamma minus academically. Moral behaviour ditto. . . .' She cast the sheet aside. 'Finkelbaum, Ephraim. Outstanding intellect, but see involvement with ffrench-Winifred, Hubert.' She threw that down too. 'Butley, Basil, recommended to G for special work with Force Q on account of brilliant performance in rugger cuppers, also forceful leadership during anti-Fascist riots. See Dean's special report. . . .'

'OK,' said Bognor. 'You've made your point.' There was a cavernous, shiny leather armchair next to a large, drooping aspidistra and Bognor sat down in it heavily, sighed, and passed a hand over a surprisingly sweaty brow.

'I presume he's got what we wanted?' he said.

Hermione was on her hands and knees trying to sort through the former contents of the filing cabinets. 'Difficult to be certain,' she said. 'Everything's such a mess. He used to file by year with a complicated cross-reference system to moral tutors and coded indexes. He half explained it to me once, but it was so abstruse I think he'd forgotten it himself.' She got to her feet and began to examine the cabinets themselves. 'Looks like it,' she said at last, forlornly. 'No sign of your year at all, Simon. We can check it out more thoroughly in the morning, but I'm afraid our murderer's got away with some nicely incriminating evidence.'

'Pity,' said Bognor. 'I should like to have seen my entry.'

'That I doubt,' said Mitten. 'It would have made salutary reading. But that's by the way. I don't understand how this could have happened. I mean, who could have got in without us knowing?'

'Not exactly Fort Knox,' Hermione snorted. 'Any halfwit could have picked these locks.'

'But,' protested Mitten, 'you have to get into the college in the first place. There's only one way in.'

'Rubbish,' said Bognor. 'There are a hundred and one climbable drainpipes to my certain knowledge. And even if he did come through the main gate, those porters are always asleep or half-cut. Or both.'

'I don't think that's fair.' Mitten pouted. 'College security has always been very strict.'

'Don't be absurd.' Hermione ran long fingers through her autumn gold hair. 'Question is, *who*?'

'Rook,' said Bognor. 'I'm almost positive Rook's file was dynamite. My information is that he only got his first because he snitched a look at the political theory paper weeks before it happened.'

'He what?' Frinton and Mitten looked at him incredulously.

'He got hold of the political theory paper in advance of the exam. Found it in this very room, no less. Was surprised by the Master, who kept mum. Accessory after the fact.'

'Not possible,' said Mitten.

Hermione Frinton ignored him. 'Why didn't you tell us before?'

'Before what?' Bognor treated the question rhetorically and continued at once. 'I couldn't tell you before anything. I only found out this evening and you were so bloody anxious to get me on the back of that absurd velocipede of yours that there was no chance to provide you with new and exciting information. If only you hadn't been so unforgivably impetuous.'

'Good grief!' she exclaimed. 'You mean to say this is some drunken tittle-tattle you've picked up over dinner with that raddled old floosie you came weaving home with just now? Do me a favour.'

Bognor glared.

Hermione Frinton glared.

Waldegrave Mitten blinked from one to the other.

Finally Bognor said, in his most theatrical manner, 'I've had a long day and I am going home to bed. No, thank you, I don't want a lift. I would rather walk. I'll see myself out.'

And he did.

5

It did not take Bognor long to walk back to the Randolph this time. Anger sped his steps, and evaporated his fatigue. He was extremely cross, not to say insulted. He objected to implications of incompetence, no matter where they came from. In the case of Parkinson they were to be expected. Parkinson's disdainful misgivings were a cross to bear, a running sore with which he had just about learned to live. Monica's gentle teasing was founded on friendship, even love, or so he believed. But this was quite different – a brand-new colleague accusing him of unprofessional conduct in front of his old tutor. And not any old brand-new colleague, but one he rather fancied. It was a bit much.

It was particularly thick because the more he thought about it the more suspicious Rook became. He had always been a flash Harry, too clever by half, always playing games with his friends' emotions and loyalties, playing a game with life itself but not the sort of game Bognor wanted to join. Rook played like a professional, always calculating the next move, interested only in winning, not in taking part, happy to foul if it was necessary. Molly Mortimer's allegations were shocking but, now that Bognor thought about them, entirely in character. Naturally Humphrey Rook would cheat. Who could have thought otherwise? The only real surprise was the Master's complicity, but Bognor could see how that had happened. To have shopped Rook at the time would have meant blackening his character and ruining his career. Beckenham would not have enjoyed that. It would have made him seem callous, particularly as part of the blame was his for leaving the exam paper lying around in such a careless manner. And Rook *was* a favourite son. It would have seemed much the easiest way out. Successful men, in Bognor's experience, always knew when to turn the blind eye. No reason to suppose that Beckenham was not perfectly Nelsonian in this respect.

If it hadn't been for his cheating Rook would probably have got a third-class degree, just like Bognor. Had Bognor cheated he would, given his luck, have been found out. This thought made him still angrier, so that as he came swinging into the Randolph's lobby the fury was rising off him like steam. Even the most unobservant and casual bystander would have noticed that they were in the presence of a very angry man indeed.

Nor did his rage abate as he ascended to his room. Had it not been for Molly Mortimer, he might have been heading bedwards with Hermione Frinton. Had it not been for Hermione Frinton, he might have been heading bedwards with Molly Mortimer. This was, of course, the purest fantasy, for despite his lascivious imaginings Bognor never went to bed with anyone but the faithful Monica. Nevertheless in matters of sex, as in practically everything else, Bognor was a fantasist, and as he moved towards a solitary bed in the cavernous hotel he found the prospect not so much depressing as enraging. In other bedrooms about the place there would, he knew full well, be endless energetic and adulterous couplings, regretted at breakfast perhaps, but not in the act. There, but for the grace of God, went he. Dammit!

So cross was he and, of course, not yet sober, that he fumbled with his key in the door and was unable to open it for a full thirty seconds. He was also insufficiently himself to notice that the light was on. Even if he had noticed, he would merely have assumed that he had left it on before going out. He had no memory for such trivia at the best of times (which this, indubitably, was not) and would never have recalled his scrupulous switching off of lights immediately before meeting Molly in the bar. If he had, he would probably have assumed that the chambermaid had left it on while turning down his bed, and so he would have been just as unsuspecting as, in fact, he was. So that under no circumstances would he have avoided the blow which caught him sharply and adroitly on the back of the head as he finally effected an entry to his room.

He slept soundly but dreamed vividly until shortly before five o'clock. The dreams were confused but exciting. In all of them he was being chased, though the identity of the pursuer was not always clear. Often the chase was processional. He would be racing across some windswept moor, with Professor Aveline bicycling behind him and gaining by the yard. Behind the professor came Molly Mortimer on horseback and behind her Hermione Frinton on Bolislav. Behind them the chief-inspector, Parkinson and Waldegrave Mitten in an open Mercedes of the type favoured by Goering. Behind them Monica, armed with a machine gun, flying through the air like Wonderwoman with some mechanized hang-gliding contrivance strapped to her torso. In other dreams he was hunted by Vole, Crutwell, Edgware and Rook, the four of them baying for him like hounds after a fox. He was always being pursued except for one particularly vivid dream, a replay of his oldest and least favourite, the nightmare in which he was once again forced to sit all thirteen papers of his final examinations at Oxford. Decked out in 'sub fusc' of gown and white bow tie, he faced the ordeal with a mind of complete blankness, an impenetrable fog of ignorance, which led to his handing in papers without a word written on them. It was a peculiarly dreadful dream and in this version it culminated in a horrific interview with Lord Beckenham, flanked by Mitten and Aveline, attended by Vole, Crutwell, Edgware and Rook. Lord Beckenham was wearing the full rig of a Lord Justice, complete with wig, and after delivering an interminable catalogue of various awfulnesses he finally donned a black cap and announced with due solemnity: 'It is therefore the sentence of this court, that you be taken from this place and hanged by the neck. . . .' At which point Bognor woke, bathed in sweat and shouting. He was lying on the carpet. For a moment he experienced that shock of complete disorientation which one always experiences on waking in a strange place.

He was so confused that for a joyous instant he was even under the impression that he felt quite well. But when he tried to move he realized that he was not only damaged, but damaged fore and aft. Part of the pain was self-inflicted, the chemical consequence of excess alcohol ingestion. Bearable in isolation, but not when taken in tandem with the physical assault inflicted by whatever outside agency had hit him on the skull with a blunt object. It was one thing to have a hammering sensation *inside* the head; it was another thing to have a hammering sensation on the *outside* of the head; but it was something of an altogether different dimension when one was being hammered inside and out. He decided to lie very still and see if he could collect his thoughts, such as they were.

'Hangover,' he said to himself hoarsely and out loud. Dimly he remembered the cognac. And the wine. And the Scotch. But if this was a hangover, why was he lying in the middle of the carpet? He frowned and wished immediately that he had not. Frowning was agony. Hangovers were an occupational hazard of the Bognor life, and as such they were instantly recognizable. Nor was drink on its own enough to floor him. It was ages since he had passed out from boozing. Not for, oh, twenty years or more. In fact he couldn't remember keeling over from alcohol since that time after the Arkwright and Blennerhasset dinner when he had drunk a bottle of port. He smiled at the memory and let out a shrill gasp of anguish. Consider the corpse on the carpet, he mused, he frowns not, neither shall he smile. Better dead than this. Very gingerly he moved his right hand to the top right-hand corner of his head and tried touching it. Not a good idea. The merest dab produced an appalling sensation as if a demon acupuncturist was playing darts with his scalp.

It was then that the telephone sounded. It made him jerk violently, as if he had shocked himself on a faulty piece of electrical wiring. This induced a wracking spasm of pain, and each subsequent ring sent further slashing knifestrokes into his defenceless brain. It was no good just lying there on the floor, much as he wanted to. It would, he knew, be agonizing to get to his feet and blunder across to the telephone, but the searing rings of the instrument had a horribly insistent sound. They were not going to go away, and if he went on lying on the floor he would shortly expire. If he made a dash for it death might well ensue, but death would at least come swiftly.

He inhaled deeply, braced himself for the effort and lunged

across the room towards the offending shrill. He succeeded in lifting the receiver from its cradle and put it to his ear, expecting to hear the voice of his unloved boss. For once he was wrong. It was not Parkinson who spoke. Instead an inspector called.

'Is that Simon Bognor?' To Bognor's tortured hearing Smith's voice sounded alarmingly gloomy.

'Yes,' he croaked. 'Simon Bognor speaking.' Each syllable hurt.

The policeman's voice seemed to falter. 'Are you all right?' he asked, a barely discernible note of sympathy twanging over the wires.

'No.' Bognor considered expanding on this, but decided against it. Words equalled effort equalled acute discomfort. He had been kneeling by the bed up to this moment, and now hauled himself to his feet and succeeded in sitting down on it. As he did he let out a moan of anguish.

'Bognor? You there? You all right?'

Bognor gritted his teeth and tried speaking through them. 'No. Half-dead. Someone tried to kill me.'

The inspector swore. 'I'm sending a car round,' he said.

'What, now?' Bognor wanted to sleep. Die, even. Mind and body screamed out for oblivion.

'In ten minutes. They'll be with you by four at the latest.'

'Four!' Bognor groaned. 'A car at four in the morning?'

Smith sounded relentless, no trace of compassion now. Perhaps he suspected a hangover, or some form of hallucination. 'It's necessary, I'm afraid. Can't say too much over the phone. And stay out of trouble. Don't answer the door to anyone except my men. I don't want a third death on my hands. Not before breakfast.'

'A *third* death?'

'Ten minutes,' said the inspector. 'I'll see you later.' And he snapped down the receiver and cut off the call with a brutal finality which Bognor, eyes closed, could visualize all too easily. Trouble, trouble, trouble, he moaned to himself. He sat slumped on the bed and tried to work out who could be dead. It was a distressing tendency in Bognor's cases for a second death to follow a first within hours or at least days of his beginning inquiries. His natural and strong inclination was to maintain that this was simply coincidence. Neverthe-less he had read his Koestler and had enough natural scepticism to be worried by persistent coincidence. He had to confess, at least to Monica and himself, that coincidence was a facile explanation. This was something worse. It had, he was very much afraid, something to do with cause and effect.

He had seldom felt worse. Fruitless to catalogue those occasions which might compete. In the past he had nearly always had the opportunity to sleep off the worst of this kind of disaster, but now he was to be jerked in an untimely manner from his sleep and forced to contemplate a corpse. Thank heaven he had remembered the Alka Seltzer. It was on the glass shelf above the washbasin, and with another superhuman effort he staggered to it and switched on the fluorescent strip light above the shaving mirror. A mistake. The face that blinked back at him was a deeply distressing apparition. Blood had run down one side and stained the skin. His hair around the temple was clotted with the stuff, and tufts of carpet adhered to his cheek and chin.

Apart from the dried red blood, some broken veins and the odd pimple, his face was a drained yellow colour. Seeing such a face on another man's body, Bognor would have crossed the road and passed by on the other side. As it was, he squinted at it through half-closed, puffy-lidded eyes. There was nothing he could say about it, he decided after a moment's frantic contemplation, and so very carefully, in order not to jerk and thereby risk further harm, he decanted a handful of white Alka Seltzer tablets into a glass of water. Leaving them to fizz for a few seconds, he turned the cold tap on full blast and, still moving with the deliberation of a man on his penultimate legs, he lowered his head into the basin and let it remain there, sighing spasmodically as the cold water splashed about it. Eventually he straightened and quaffed the Alka Seltzer, trying not to look himself in the eye. Then, thinking that perhaps he was feeling marginally less ghastly, he ventured a glance at the image in the glass. Less blood than before, but otherwise enough to turn the least squeamish stomach. He pulled at the knot of his Arkwright and Blennerhasset tie, then dabbed at the blood with a dampened face towel. His head was still leaking under the hair, but the blood which must have flowed quite freely at first was now merely oozing. Everything still hurt like hell, but before long the Alka Seltzer might take some of the edge off the damage. He wondered if he needed stitches. Probably. Would he be able to stay conscious? Perhaps. Who was the second corpse? Molly Mortimer? Hermione Frinton? Waldy Mitten? Maybe an Apocrypha scholarship candidate, thwarted by the examining body, was going to knock off the Senior Common Room one by one. Oh for Codes and Ciphers! Oh for home and Monica! If the police were going to be ten minutes arriving he might just have time for a quick lie-down. He made his way back to the bed and sprawled on it, face down. . . .

He was woken immediately, though so deep was the oblivion to which he succumbed as soon as his head touched the counterpane that he felt as if he had been asleep for weeks. The banging on the door provoked a dream at first and, waking, Bognor was surprised to find himself protesting in Shakespearean tones he had not used since his last term at school: 'Knock, knock, knock! Who's there in the name of Beelzebub?'

At which there was a pause before a voice, at once officious and subordinate, shouted back, 'Police, sir. Constable Atkinson. Come from Inspector Smith.'

Bognor frowned. The inspector had said he was sending a car round, but he had also warned Bognor against opening the door to any but his own men. How could he know whether this Constable Atkinson was the real thing, or the failed assassin returned to finish the job off properly?

'Who do you want?' asked Bognor cautiously.

'Mr Bognor of the Board of Trade, sir. Is that you, Mr Bognor?'

Bognor's head throbbed. This was silly. 'Look,' he said. 'Even if it is me, your Inspector Smith warned me not to let anyone in except you. If you are you. Do you have any ID?'

Another pause. A shuffling, a rustling and then the sound of someone fiddling with the bottom of the door. A moment later a plastic-coated card slid underneath it and lay on the carpet. 'ID, sir,' said the voice. 'I think you'll find it in order.'

Bognor knelt, not without difficulty and discomfort, and

managed to scoop the card off the floor. It revealed, as expected, that its owner was, Detective-Constable Atkinson of the local CID. Bognor accordingly opened up, to find himself staring at a burly, red-faced man with bushy eyebrows, a Donegal tweed jacket, grey flannel trousers and brown brogues.

On seeing Bognor this worthy took two smart steps back and removed his hands from his pockets. 'Crippen!' he exclaimed, evidently using the famous murderer's name as an expression of astonishment. He did not seem to Bognor to be suggesting that he *was* Crippen, nor even that Bognor was a latter-day victim of the doctor. It was simply an expletive.

Bognor smiled weakly, glad of creating such an instant and dramatic effect. It did not often happen. In fact quite often he was not noticed at all until things started to go wrong and Parkinson produced him as a scapegoat. The smile was not much of a success. Scarcely worth the effort.

'Stone the crows!' continued the constable. 'What you been doing?'

Bognor indicated his head, dabbing at the wound just above the temple. His fingers came away bloody and he gazed at them thoughtfully for a moment before showing them to the policeman.

'Jesus,' said Constable Atkinson, glancing rapidly to left and right, and at the same time slipping a hand to his hip and producing an ugly black revolver. With his other hand he pushed Bognor back into the room. Once inside he replaced the gun and examined Bognor's injury. 'That's not at all nice, sir, if I might say so. Whoever did that was taking quite a risk, or he didn't know what he was about. Could have killed you, that could. Can you walk?'

'I can try,' muttered Bognor.

'Ought to take you straight round to Casualty,' said Atkinson sympathetically. 'Only I'm afraid that's a little luxury the chief isn't going to allow us.' He looked at his watch. '*Donner und Blitzen*,' he said unexpectedly. 'We're late as it is. But we've got a first-aid kit in the car and I'll find something to put on it, even if it's only some antiseptic and a strip of Band-Aid. Who did it? Any idea?'

'None,' said Bognor ruefully. 'Jumped me the second I

opened the door.'

Atkinson glanced round the room. 'Looking for something,' he said, gesturing towards the drawers and cupboards, all of which were open.

Bognor simply had not noticed. Even now he was not sure whether the whirlwind effect, the scattered clothing, the ransacked drawers and the confetti of papers were the result of interlopers or of his own untidiness.

'Any idea what?'

'What what?'

'What they were looking for?'

'None. Nor who.'

'Who?

'Yes, "who". Who hit me on the head. No idea who.'

'Oh.' Atkinson rubbed his chin and stared around him at the debris. 'Anything missing?' he asked.

'Dunno,' said Bognor, truthfully but unhelpfully.

Atkinson glanced at him sharply and decided that this was best pursued at some later date. 'May be some brandy in the car,' he said, pleasantly.

'Ugh.' Bognor retched and shuddered. 'Anything but brandy,' he said.

The detective-constable frowned. 'Best be going, sir, if you can manage it.'

Bognor told him, unconvincingly, that he could manage perfectly well, but after a few steps it was clear that he needed official support. They made most of the journey arm in arm and passed through the lobby like a couple in post-coital euphoria, causing the hall porter to raise his eyebrows, suck his teeth, shake his head and observe, *sotto voce*, that he didn't know what the place was coming to and that young gentlemen had ceased being young gentlemen many years ago.

Outside, the white police Rover was parked on the double yellow line, engine running, blue light flashing. Atkinson guided Bognor into the back seat, then got in alongside the driver. The car shot forward like a greyhound from the traps, ramming Bognor's stomach against his spine.

'Oh well,' he gasped as he slumped into the upholstery. 'Better than Bolislav.'

'I beg your pardon, sir?' Atkinson turned, sympathetically.

He had found the first-aid kit and was rummaging about in it, searching for sticking plaster.

'Motorbike,' said Bognor, grinning queasily. 'I was on one earlier. Took the breath away.'

Atkinson smiled uneasily. 'I see, sir. Now, if you wouldn't mind just leaning forward a bit, I'll have a go at cleaning up that cut and sticking something over it.'

But even as he said it Bognor's eyes closed, his mouth fell open and he slipped away into the release of sleep. Atkinson regarded him briefly to see if he was breathing, was reassured by the onslaught of stentorian snores, and turned back to face the front.

'Not in a good way, poor sod,' he said to his colleague.

'What happened to him?'

'Had a skinful, went home to bed and got hit on the head with a blunt instrument. Not so blunt it didn't cut him, though. Table lamp probably, unless whoever done it was carrying a cosh. Amateur, whoever it was. Messy.'

They drove on in silence, speeding along the deserted road through north Oxford, along the bypass, turning off on a minor road and then, still travelling at a reckless clip which would have terrified Bognor had he been awake, they passed through a trio of dormant, picturesque country villages of the type favoured by weekenders from London and the richer, trendier Oxford dons. In a fourth, even more picturesquely postcard than the others, they turned left by the church and down a lane which, after a mile or so, became little more than a muddy track. They climbed for a few minutes, rattled over a cattle grid, and parked a hundred yards further on where several vehicles already stood and where the night was illuminated by lights and torches. As they halted, the be-mackintoshed figure of Inspector Smith was caught in the beam of the headlights, and Bognor woke.

His first coherent vision was of the inspector easing into the rear seat alongside him.

'Bad business,' he said.

Bognor did not reply.

'Anyway, can't be helped. Just have to hope there's a silver lining. How are *you*?' He snapped on the interior light and caught his breath as he saw Bognor properly. 'Sorry I asked,' he said after a moment. He felt in the pocket of his mac and pulled out a hip flask. 'Here,' he said. 'Brandy. You look as if you could use it.'

Bognor gagged and turned his head away.

'Suit yourself,' said the inspector, taking a swig himself before putting the flask back in his pocket. 'So someone had a go at you, eh?'

Bognor nodded.

'Any idea who?'

Bognor shook his head.

'When did this happen?'

Bognor said he couldn't be sure, but it must have been between eleven and twelve. Or so he supposed. The inspector nodded at this and gave an impression of thought. When he had finished he said, 'Perfectly possible for whoever did for our friend over there to have got back in time to have a go at you, too.'

'When . . . ?' began Bognor, then checked himself. 'I mean who was it?'

'Time of death estimated at somewhere around seven or eight yesterday evening,' replied Smith, 'in answer to the first part of your question. As for the second, you'd better come and have a look. He hasn't been moved yet and the only identification so far is from his driving licence and credit cards. Since he was a friend of yours you'd better do the honours. Can you walk?'

'Up to a point.'

'It's not far.'

They both got out of the car and Bognor stood for a second, testing the springy upland turf.

'Bit of luck finding him this quick,' said Smith conversationally. 'This couple came up for a quick spot of how's your father and just fell over him. Bad luck on them, I'm afraid. Both of them playing away from home, if you know what I mean. Not that there's anything unusual about that in this day and age. There'll be trouble, though. University types they were. Told their respective spouses they were going to choir practice. Ha!' He laughed coldly. 'The Almighty moves in mysterious ways, his wonders to perform, don't you think?'

There was a heavy dew underfoot and it soaked through Bognor's suedes, moistening his socks. To his already frightful physical condition he now added a dryness of the throat and a tightening of the stomach. Something to do with apprehension. Collecting his thoughts was out of the question. He could not even begin to guess whose body was lying out here on the hillside, stumbled upon by an adulterous courting couple. What a way to go. For himself he wanted to die in bed, preferably at once.

Some sort of bivouac had been placed over the dead person, and as they reached it Smith pulled aside the end and shone his torch in, illuminating the man's face. Bognor, braced for the shock, stared in, gulped, swallowed hard and turned away. Smith caught him as he half fell and forced some of the contents of his flask down his throat. This time Bognor was almost grateful for it, but after taking it he broke away from Smith and took a few steps into the darkness. He wanted to be alone and for a short while the policeman granted the unspoken wish. Then, all too soon, he was at his elbow again.

'Sorry about that,' he said. 'Friend of yours, was he?'

'It's not that,' said Bognor. 'Only I'm afraid that in a manner of speaking it's my fault. I should have bloody well listened. Damn! Damn! Damn!' He pulled out a spotted handkerchief and blew his nose loudly.

'The documents,' said Inspector Smith, 'lead us to suppose that the deceased is one Sebastian Vole.'

'Yes,' said Bognor softly. 'That's Vole all right.'

6

Bognor sat on the back seat of the Rover with his head between his knees and moaned softly. It was idle to pretend that he had ever numbered the dead man among his nearest and dearest, but their acquaintanceship went back to days of callow youth, wine and roses, salad days, carefree this and that and what have you. And that meant something. Bognor did not exactly weep for Vole, but he did allow himself a little stiff-upper-lipped keening. Of all his contemporaries, Vole was the only one who remembered Christmas. Every year the card came without fail: 'Season's Greetings from Prendergast History Faculty' and, in green ink, the spikily executed words 'Sebastian Vole'. Of all his brilliant contemporaries Vole had been the most, well, human. Vole stayed up all night playing poker. Vole liked a drink. Vole had been sick over the Junior Proctor one night after an Arkwright and Blennerhasset meeting. Vole was all right. And now, alas, poor Vole, he lay stiff and cold on an Oxfordshire hillside. This *had* been a professional job. Hands tied, blindfolded. A single shot from close range in the back of the neck.

'It's my fault,' moaned Bognor again. 'If only I'd listened.'

Smith, who was standing outside, leaning against the open window, sympathized with his colleague's pain and grief but was becoming bored by this incomprehensible refrain. Now that he had heard it half a dozen times he decided he could seek elucidation without seeming callous.

'What was it,' he asked kindly, 'that he told you?'

'About his book,' moaned Bognor. 'He was right all the time. Just because he made such an ass of himself with Mussolini I didn't believe him. But he was right. Dammit, he was right, and look where it got him. Shot in the back by that

Kremlin sociologist. God, this country's going to the dogs!'

The inspector took another swig from his flask and frowned. He had lost the thread of his colleague's remarks.

'Come again,' he said helpfully. 'I'm not quite with you.'

'We *all* mocked him,' said Bognor. 'But *he* was right and *we* were wrong.'

'But what did he tell you?'

'He told me he was on to Professor Aveline.'

'What, *the* Professor Aveline? Professor Max Aveline? The Regius Professor of Sociology?'

'The same.'

The inspector cleared his throat noisily. An ambulance had arrived and they were taking Vole away. Bognor watched in the grey half-light of early morning. There was a damp mist shrouding the hillside. The men's breath steamed. He was reminded of the last dawn he had seen, no time at all ago, the morning after the gaudy, the morning Lord Beckenham walked home to his death. And now Vole.

'And what do you mean when you say he was "on" to Aveline? You're too quick for me, I'm afraid. I'm only a poor policeman. Don't have the benefits of a varsity education like you.'

Bognor didn't like people who said varsity. It reminded him of Betjeman: 'I'm afraid the fellows in Putney rather wish they had/The social ease and manners of a varsity undergrad.' And thinking of Betjeman Bognor remembered another of the Laureate's verses, bleaker lines on the death of some old fellow of Pembroke: 'The body waits in Pembroke College where the ivy taps the panes/All night.' And then: 'Those old cheeks that faintly flushed as the port suffused the veins,/Drain'd white.' Beckenham, Vole . . . no more port for either of them. Both drained whiter than white. Vanished as if they had never been. Would Vole's manuscript be published after death? Could you be awarded a posthumous All Souls Fellowship? Would justice be done? And seen to be done?

'I hate to hurry you.' The policeman meant the exact opposite of what he said. Chivvying people along was what he liked best in all the world. If Bognor had been a suspect and not a colleague he might have hit him about a bit in the cause of truth. The thought passed through both men's minds.

'Sorry,' said Bognor, not meaning it either. 'I had a long talk with Vole yesterday. He made me promise not to say anything about it for forty-eight hours.'

'As the result of which . . .' said the inspector. Unnecessarily, Bognor thought.

'It was supremely important to him,' he snapped. 'You could say that his life's work depended on it.'

'Life too, come to that.'

'Yes, well.'

Another protracted silence ensued, and then Bognor told Inspector Smith about his conversation with Vole. Smith did not comment until the story was complete, and even then he waited while he dragged out a battered briar pipe, stuffed it full of shag and lit it clumsily. 'Can't say,' he said at last, between spluttering puffs, 'I'm surprised you took it with a pinch of salt. Not a likely story.'

'That's what I thought,' said Bognor. 'If this were Cambridge it would be different, but I've always assumed that sort of thing couldn't happen here.'

'So you're saying Aveline tied him up, blindfolded him, shot him and then drove out here and dumped him?'

Bognor pondered. Aveline may have been amazingly virile for his age, but his age was considerable. It seemed unlikely that he could have dealt so effectively with even a drunken Vole.

'He'd have needed help.'

'And,' Smith blew a cloud of Auld Reekie in Bognor's direction, 'you're thinking what I'm thinking.'

'Which is?' Bognor was not going to be caught out like that.

'That if he's who Vole thought he was, then he'd know precisely where to go for that sort of help.'

'Quite.'

'Next question is, can we prove it?' The inspector puffed away thoughtfully.

'Don't see why not,' said Bognor. 'If Vole left all his notes and working papers at Prendergast, that should give us enough evidence to smoke Aveline out. Besides, if he really was working for the Russians all these years, someone must have had *some* sort of an idea.'

'I wouldn't bet on it,' said Smith. 'Anyway, I think we should strike while the iron's hot. Almost time for breakfast. Let's take a coffee and some toast off the Regius Professor.'

Smith slid into the back seat alongside Bognor who, on the point of vomiting, asked him to extinguish the pipe. He did, and the car moved away down the hill some five minutes behind the ambulance carrying Vole's corpse to the mortuary. There was a phone box in the village and Smith decided they should stop there to find Aveline's address in the directory. When they got there, however, they discovered that the phone book was missing.

'I'll try Directory Inquiries,' said Smith, asking Bognor for a 10p coin. Bognor had no such thing, so walked to the car and borrowed one from Constable Atkinson. When he got back he said, 'He's bound to be ex-directory. No point trying. I'll call Waldegrave Mitten. He'll know.' He glanced at his watch, which showed him it was not long after six. It would be satisfying to telephone Mitten at this ungodly hour. He was certain to be asleep, having no more love for the early morning than Bognor himself.

It took him no little time to persuade the college porter of the importance of his request, but eventually he was put through to the acting Master's rooms. The bell rang several times before an aggrieved, strangulated voice said, 'Do you know what bloody time it is?'

'About six-fifteen, actually,' said Bognor. 'But it *is* important. Very. I'm afraid we've had another death.'

'Who is this?'

'Bognor,' said Bognor. 'Bognor, Board of Trade. That *is* Waldegrave Mitten, isn't it?'

'Oh, it's you,' said Mitten with an air of resignation. 'Could you ring back in an hour? It's not, er, convenient.'

'Convenience doesn't come into it.' Bognor spoke with asperity. 'I need Aveline's address. There's been another death.'

'If Aveline's dead, you hardly need his address.'

'Aveline's not dead. It's someone else. I can't talk about it on the phone.'

'You're not making sense,' protested Mitten. 'In fact you sound like one of your essays. If someone else is dead, why do you need Aveline's address?'

'Listen,' said Bognor, 'this is not something I can talk about over the phone, but I do assure you it's vital. Please may I have Aveline's address?'

'He has a flat in Norham Gardens,' said Mitten, 'but I happen to know he's not there.'

Bognor sighed. 'I've only got one 10p piece,' he said, 'and we're going to run out of time in a moment. I'm not at all well, a man is dead and I must know where Professor Aveline is.'

'He's at his cottage,' said Mitten, 'but I can't give you the address. He's most particular about it. It's his hideaway. He'd kill me if I gave it to you.'

'Since he's killed at least one man already I should think that's very much on the cards,' said Bognor drily. 'You don't seem to realize we're investigating a murder. Two murders in point of fact. You're obstructing us in our inquiries. That's an offence.'

Mitten was manifestly exasperated, but after some ritual huffing, puffing and minatory muttering he said, 'Oh, very well then, but I want you to know that I do this under protest. Also that under no circumstances are you to tell Max how you found out.'

'No, no, of course not. . . . Just tell me where it is.'

A pause. 'The Old Bakehouse, Compton Courtenay. It's about ten miles outside Oxford.'

'Thanks very much,' he said. 'You can go back to sleep now.' And he replaced the receiver noisily.

'Compton Courtenay,' he said to the inspector, squeezed up against him in the kiosk.

'Ah,' said the inspector, a glint coming into his eyes. 'Now that *is* a piece of luck.'

Bognor caught a heavy whiff of armpit, whisky and stale tobacco. Quickly he opened the door and tumbled out.

'Luck?' he inquired from the soggily bracing safety of the great outdoors.

'Luck, laddie. Look!' The inspector jabbed a finger at the code on the dial: 'Compton Courtenay 2246 X,' he said, triumphantly. 'We're in bloody Compton Courtenay already.'

'Oh,' said Bognor. 'That *is* good news. All we have to do now is find the Old Bakehouse. Then we can sit down and have a jolly little breakfast with Mad Max the Murderous Marxist.'

'Sorry,' said the inspector. 'Forgot you were feeling a degree or two under. You want to get stitched up and have a kip? Nothing much you can do at the moment, and I can get a car to drive you into Casualty at the Radcliffe.'

'No, thanks,' said Bognor. 'Let's go and collect the Professor first. Always assuming he's still there. Are you armed?'

Smith nodded. 'Atkinson and the others, too.' He jerked his head towards the second car which was stopped just outside the Belt and Braces public house.

'Not that you need to worry about that,' he went on. 'If he did murder your friend Vole, the odds are that he'll have scarpered. On the other hand, if he's still in bed then he's innocent.'

'That sounds a bit simple,' said Bognor. 'How do you work that out?'

'Common sense . . . experience . . . and a feel for the job,' said Inspector Smith, managing to suggest that these essential qualifications were not shared by his colleague from the Board of Trade. 'Come on! Let's go. Aren't more than about a dozen houses to choose from.'

This was correct. A hundred years ago and more this would have been a small feudal village owned by the local lord and peopled by his tenants and workers. Now, however, the local lord was reduced to living in the west wing while the paying public had the run of the rest of the house. The workers were all in council estates on the edge of Oxford or Thame. The only people who lived in Compton Courtenay were regius professors of sociology and company directors. The Regius Professor's abode was the third house they came to, a ducky little stone and thatched number with roses and honeysuckle round the porch, staddlestones by the front path, heavily leaded windows and a strong suspicion of *House and Garden* exposed beam and Aga. Very Volvo and Brie, as the Americans would have it.

Bognor, unarmed as usual, lurked in the background, nursing his wounds, aches and self-recrimination while the constabulary fanned out to cover all possible entrances and exits. Smith, as befitted the man in charge, made purposefully for the front door and banged the heavy iron knocker loudly, three times. There being no answer, he tried again. After a third effort he took out a handgun, motioned two policemen to cover him, and turned the door handle. The door opened. Standing back, the inspector gave it a kick, and waited. Bognor, watching, decided that his colleague chappie was more nervous than he liked to admit.

The early morning silence was broken by the church clock striking the quarter. The door, under the impact of the inspector's kick, swung wide open and then, very slowly and with a slight creak, swung back. The inspector pushed it open with his hand this time and entered. Behind him followed the two policemen. Bognor, for reasons he preferred not to examine – they would have had too much to do with extreme caution, not to say fear – remained outside. About five minutes later the inspector emerged.

'Done a bunk,' he shouted. 'Come on in. The other two are making coffee.'

Bognor did as he was asked, feeling too like a trespasser for comfort. He wiped his feet fastidiously on the mat and found himself in a long, low living-room with stairs leading to the upper storey. Two rooms and a passage had obviously been knocked into one. By the surprisingly chintzy, high-backed armchairs there were empty glasses and two ashtrays with several butts in them. The grate contained ash. Yesterday's *Guardian* lay open on a window seat, and on the dining-table at the far end of the room a cut-glass jug half full of water sat next to a bottle of Dimple Haig whisky with about an inch left in the bottom. The room smelt faintly pub-like, tobacco and alcohol mixing with more animal smells. Although it was messy, there were no signs of a struggle.

The inspector rubbed his hands together, making a rasping sound with the palms. 'Done a bunk,' he said again. 'Shaving things missing from the bathroom. Drawers opened. Left in a hurry. Didn't even wash up or lock the door behind him.'

'People don't lock front doors in the country.'

'Call this country?' said the inspector sceptically. 'Should

110

be prints on the glasses. Neighbours may have noticed something.'

Constable Atkinson appeared, bearing hot Nescafé in Portmeirion pottery mugs. Bognor shovelled three spoonfuls of sugar into his and drank it black. 'Open and shut,' he said.

'Oh, yes?' The inspector cocked an eyebrow. 'Enlighten me.'

'OK.' Bognor took a deep breath. 'Vole has all the evidence necessary to prove that Aveline was the Kremlin's top Briton. "Made Philby look like an office boy" were his words, if I remember correctly. So he asks Aveline for an interview. Aveline naturally knows that Vole's been on the trail for years, and he realizes that he's finally caught up with him. He has to make sure, of course. He knows Vole didn't really do his homework on the Mussolini book, so there's a chance he's been careless again. But Aveline is worried.' Bognor sipped the sickly-sweet brew and mopped his forehead. He wondered if he should bother to get his wound stitched. 'So rather than risk exposure in the twilight of his days,' he continued, 'he gets on to his friends and asks them to send up one of their high-powered heavies to help him out if things go wrong. Vole arrives, slightly pissed. Boris sits in on the interview. It very quickly becomes apparent that Vole knows chapter and verse, so Boris pulls a gun, trusses poor old Vole up like poultry and bundles him away to a quiet spot where he shoots him and dumps him. Meanwhile Aveline, as you put it, does a bunk and Boris goes back to Millionaires' Row where he doubtless masquerades as a third secretary (cultural).'

'Yes.' Smith seemed weary. 'I'll buy that as far as it goes. In which case Aveline could be in Moscow by now, though I'll put out a call just in case. He's probably had twelve hours, and with the resources at his disposal any one of a number of passports. Trouble is, I don't see that any of this gets us any further.'

'What do you mean . . . "further"?'

'I mean,' said the inspector, 'that this murder inquiry began with the death of Lord Beckenham of Penge. Am I right?'

'You are right.'

111

'And we still don't know who did that.'

'We don't?'

'*I* don't.'

Bognor pursed his lips. 'Beckenham was a stooge of Aveline's. One of what will no doubt turn out to have been a complex network of moles and agents and fifth columnists. As soon as Beckenham was approached by Vole he would have consulted Aveline. Aveline would have been worried that Beckenham would spill the beans, and so he knocks him off before Vole can get at him. QED.'

'Several things wrong with that,' said Smith. 'One: lack of opportunity. How did he doctor the Master's raspberry tipple? He was in his own rooms all that night until he bicycled back to his flat in north Oxford. Two: he'd have been out here with Vole when the Master's filing cabinet was being done over. And three: he'd have been on his way to Moscow when you were being hit over the head at the Randolph. All of which adds up to quite conclusive evidence that, whatever else he may have done, Professor Aveline did not kill Lord Beckenham. Not QED at all.'

'No, I suppose not. Except that he could have got someone else to do the dirty work. He got someone else to kill poor Vole.'

'But he used a pro,' said Smith. 'Whoever knocked you about was an amateur. And so was the geezer who did the Master's files. If Aveline is the kind of operator you say he is, then he'd have had more class than that.'

'So where does that leave us?' asked Bognor.

'Nowhere much,' said the inspector. 'We'll follow this one through, naturally, but all we're going to find is that it was the Professor who did it, for reasons aforementioned, and that he's got clean away. If he didn't and if he hasn't, I'm a virgin.'

Bognor nodded. 'I wish he *had* done it,' he said. 'But I agree – I don't think he did. And now, if you don't mind, I think I'd better get stitched up and have a quick kip.'

It looked as if they were right. By the time Bognor surfaced, feeling weary but human, it transpired that Aveline, using his own name, had caught the night boat from Southampton to Le Havre. By the time the inspector and Hermione Frinton had managed to get Interpol and the French security people to treat the matter with anything approaching seriousness, Aveline had vanished. This was hotly disputed by the French and some other European officials, who denied that in the latter half of the twentieth century it was possible for individuals simply to disappear into thin air. It was also claimed that border security was amazingly rigorous and foolproof, that even if the fugitive professor was able to elude the enveloping tentacles of the French dragnet he would be snaffled the second he came within sight of the border. Bognor shrugged and sighed and wondered how long it would be before some watchful Western newspaper correspondent recorded a sighting of Aveline in the crush bar at the Bolshoi, or browsing in the Hermitage. Days rather than weeks, in his opinion.

Vole's death and his own battering did have one happy side-effect, which was a reconciliation of sorts with Dr Frinton. On waking in mid-afternoon, feeling revived and even marginally peckish, he sauntered down to the lounge in search of a pot of tea and a round or two of hot buttered toast. After ordering these he checked with reception for messages (he had left the strictest imaginable instructions that he was under no circumstances whatever to be disturbed) and found, along with half a dozen increasingly angry messages from Parkinson, a note from Hermione, handwritten and presumably hand-delivered. It said: 'Sorry about last night. Your gin is still in the fridge. Potter round as soon as you recover use of your limbs. Love Hermione.'

This perked him up no end, and after consuming tea and toast with surprising enthusiasm he did indeed potter round to Dr Frinton's pad in Walton Street. He was disconcerted on arriving to find that the house appeared to be given over to something called the Vegan Brotherhood for International Peace and Harmony. In a scruffy ground-floor office a whey-faced man with long pigtails and an unkempt beard streaked with green told him that Dr Frinton lived in the attic. Bognor ascended the narrow staircase gingerly, for the carpet was threadbare and only loosely attached to *terra firma*. Some way up, further progress was barred by a door. On the left-hand side was a bell-push with the word 'Frinton' on it. Bognor pressed it and was rewarded by a metallic, disembodied, but recognizably Hermionian voice issuing from a grille above the bell-push.

'Yes?' was all she said.

'It's me,' said Bognor to the grille. 'Simon Bognor of the Board of Trade.'

'Enter, Simon Bognor of the Board of Trade. And bring in the milk if there's any there.'

Bognor could see no milk. He pushed the door open and climbed more narrow stairs, immaculately carpeted this time in chocolate haircord. Seconds later he emerged into an unexpectedly airy and almost enormous room in the middle of which Dr Frinton sat in the lotus position clad only in an emerald-green leotard with the legend 'All Souls Yoga XV' across the chest. There was a strong smell of joss stick and from the quadrophonic loudspeakers there issued the clipped, desiccated and crackling voice of T. S. Eliot reading 'The Waste Land'.

'Oh,' said Bognor backing off. 'Did I come at a bad time?'

'Not in the least, darling,' said Hermione, not moving anything except her lips, and these no more than absolutely necessary for the purpose of speech. 'Just having a quick think.'

'Ah,' said Bognor. He wandered over to the plate glass windows which ran along the entire length of the room, giving onto an elegantly pot-planted terrace and affording inimitably Oxonian vistas of spires, dreaming.

'The fridge is in the kitchen,' she said. 'You should be able to recognize the gin. It has an olive in it.'

'Thanks, I'll wait.' Books did furnish the room. They did so somewhat ostentatiously, expensive coffee table numbers jostling battered volumes from the London Library, almost certainly long overdue for return. Bognor picked up a copy of Cobb's *Tour de France* and tried to decipher the inscription which was effusive, not easily decipherable and evidently from the author himself. Bognor's French was not up to it, so he discarded it and instead gazed out of the window across the Oxford landmarks to the great green dome of Apocrypha itself. Who would have thought, all those years ago, that he would return to this of all places, to investigate this of all crimes? No one that *he* could think of.

'Right,' called Hermione, lifting the needle from the turn-table and cutting off the poet in full flight. ' "Webster was much possessed by death/And saw the skull beneath the skin." You too by the look of you, so it's time for a gin.'

'Maybe,' said Bognor gloomily.

She arched eyebrows and neck simultaneously. 'Too far gone even for the hair of the dog?'

'I'm not hung over. Someone hit me.'

'I do know, as a matter of fact. Someone hit you, but you're hung over too. Or deserve to be. You stank of alcohol, but . . .' she raised a palm *à la* traffic policeman, 'we are not going to start *that* all over again. You have suffered enough.' She grinned. 'Now I am going to change into something loose and easy and then you can tell me *all* about it. And while you're doing that why don't you do something dangerous with gin. There are some madly exotic things in the kitchen: coin-treau, grenadine, passion fruit, chinese gooseberries, even some packets of instant Singapore Sling if you're feeling lazy.' Saying which, she flounced off to what was pre-sumably the bedroom.

Bognor for his part meandered into the kitchen, which had all the hallmarks of good living but not particularly good cooking: microwave oven, potted things, expensively canned things, bottled things from Fortnum's and Fauchon, a Magimix. The smoked salmon in the fridge came from Ecclefechan. Bognor guessed that Dr Frinton liked to eat out but prided herself on being able to rustle something up at a moment's notice without leaving her guest(s) alone for more than thirty seconds at a time. Slightly lugubriously he studied the drinks and finally opted for the Singapore Sling mix. His own gin – with a splash of martini, to judge from a quick sniff – he left alone, and instead sloshed some fresh from the bottle into the blender, added almost a whole tray of ice, two sachets of crystals and some water, pressed the button and let it whoosh. It frothed into a pale pink, milk shake-like concoction which he guessed his hostess would have deftly decorated with slices of pineapple, sprigs of

poinsettia and any other vegetation to hand. He, charac-
teristically, poured it into two large tumblers, spilling a little
which he mopped up half-heartedly with a handkerchief,
being unable to locate the kitchen towels. When he had done,
he returned to the drawing-room (*salon*, he thought, was
probably a more appropriate word), glass in each hand, to
find Hermione putting the final adjustment to jangling drop
ear-rings which looked suspiciously like diamonds. She was
wearing an extremely low-cut white silk quasi-diaphanous
garment with sequins or some such all over it. These were
silver and sparkled. She smelt overpoweringly of scent,
which Bognor sensed was amazingly expensive. Inwardly he
sighed. He wished he felt more in the mood for her.

'Ah,' she said, eyeing the pink froth. 'You cheated.'

' 'fraid so,' he admitted. 'Not much of a bartender. Scotch
and soda's about my limit.'

'Consumption rather than construction?'

'You could put it like that.'

She smiled and took one of the glasses. 'Well, chin-chin,'
she said.

'Yes,' said Bognor. 'Chin-chin.' He raised his glass and
drank. It tasted very sweet and fruity. If he hadn't known, he
would have assumed it was free of alcohol.

'I was beginning to think you'd never make it,' she said.
'Come and sit down and tell me all about it.' She sank, in a
seductively flowing movement, onto the sofa and patted the
cushions in an invitation to Bognor to join her. He did, sitting
primly and uncomfortably and well away from her. After
contemplating him speculatively for a second she put her feet
up so that they rested on his lap, then she lay back and said: 'If
you're feeling particularly generous you may tickle my feet.'

'Right,' said Bognor.

'Oh, and could you be an angel and light me a cigarette?
In the box there.' She nodded towards a japanned papier
mâché object which Bognor opened to find full of Black
Russians. He lit one and passed it to her. Accepting it, she
allowed her hand to linger on his, and when she smiled a
husky thank you she looked him searchingly in the eyes, the
sexual message unmistakable. Bognor looked away, and sat
more stiffly than ever.

'I just can't think who can have done it,' he said.

'What, darling?' She exhaled very slowly, forming her lips in a tiny perfect 'o'.

'Attacked me.'

'Oh, that.'

'Yes, *that*. "That", as you put it, was exceedingly painful. I've had to have stitches.'

'How many?'

'Three, actually.'

She laughed. 'I don't call that very many.'

'It's quite enough,' he said. 'Why do you imagine it happened?'

'What do you want to know, "*Who*dunnit?" or "*Why* they dunnit?" If we know the second, we know the first.'

Bognor was beginning to be muddled.

'First of all,' she said, 'someone broke into the Master's lodgings to steal the confidential files. Particularly the ones for your year.'

'Yes.'

'Which they did.'

'Yes.'

'Then, when you return to your hotel room, it's being done over, except you're too drunk to notice.'

'I . . .'

She silenced him with a tap of her heel to the groin. 'I thought you were going to tickle my feet.'

'Oh.'

'What's the matter? Don't my feet turn you on? Some men think my feet are my sexiest feature.'

'Sorry, I'm not really into feet.'

'Tell me what you *are* into, then.' She stubbed out her cigarette and gave him a louchely come-hither smile.

'Nothing much at the moment,' conceded Bognor, 'except for solving these bloody murders.'

'Well, it wasn't me.'

'Could have been,' said Bognor. 'You had that hideous velocipede of yours. I was on foot.'

'Velocette, darling. But why should I want to hit you on the head?'

'I don't know. You were being extremely disagreeable.'

'You should see me when I try. When I'm really disagreeable I'm perfectly bloody.'

'I can imagine.'

She sipped at her drink and looked at him over the rim of the glass. 'All right,' she said. 'We'll solve the murder and then relax. I can see you aren't going to be the slightest use until you've found out who did it. For my first thesis I wish to propose that, despite any evidence to the contrary, the murder of Beckenham and the murder of Vole have nothing whatever to do with each other.'

'That's ridiculous.'

'No more ridiculous than what's happened already. The Master revealed as a Soviet agent, found murdered. An Apocrypha alumnus shot dead by the Regius Professor of Sociology's hit man. The Regius Professor turns out to be Philby with knobs on. Beats *Dallas* any day of the week.'

'And there's the small matter of the prospective Conservative candidate for Sheen Central cheating in his final exams.'

'I don't think we ought to get involved in all that again.'

Bognor sighed. 'Maybe not,' he said. 'I take your point. At the moment the place is coming apart at the seams and anything's possible. So let's suppose you're right and the two murders have nothing to do with each other. What then?'

'Then we can eliminate Aveline and Vole as suspects for the Master's murder.'

'Aveline was never a suspect for the Master's murder anyway.'

'*I* suspected him.' Hermione looked arch. She had finished her drink. 'Shall we have another?' she asked.

Bognor said he wasn't particularly thirsty. She told him not to be silly. Together they went to the kitchen.

'Are you hungry?' she asked him.

'I'm always hungry,' said Bognor, which was more or less true, though it was barely an hour since his toast and tea.

'I didn't have lunch,' said Hermione. 'What would you say to scrambled eggs with smoked salmon?'

'Yummy,' said Bognor.

'And I tell you what, there's a bottle of Veuve Clicquot I keep in the fridge for emergencies such as this. While I'm scrambling, you open that. It should clear your head. And it's better for you than gin sling.'

Bognor did as he was told. He hadn't the energy to do otherwise, though for once in his life he would just as soon have had cocoa. 'Do you think it could have been Edgware or Crutwell?' he asked, as he tried to ease the cork out without hurting anyone.

'Why Edgware or Crutwell?'

'I saw them in the High that afternoon when I was out walking with Vole. At least I think I did. They were in a bright red Range Rover. I waved at them. Funny thing was that they didn't wave back. Didn't even acknowledge me. What do you make of that?'

Hermione whisked eggs and looked pensive. 'You sure it was them?'

'Course I'm sure.'

'Mmm.'

Bognor managed to remove the cork with a gratifyingly discreet mini-burp and poured two glasses.

Hermione took a sip and went on scrambling. 'So,' she said, 'Crutwell and Edgware were in Oxford that afternoon not wanting to be noticed, and had the bad luck to run into you. But why on earth should they go to your room at the Randolph? And what were they looking for?'

'Search me,' he said.

Hermione cut off a large slab of butter and dropped it in the saucepan, then began to chop smoked salmon. 'Suppose,' she said, 'they think you've got something they want. Now what could that be?'

'Nothing. They have everything. The world is at their feet. Life is their oyster, or words to that effect. I, I who have nothing. . . . No, out of the question.'

'No, no. Try to be literal.' She added the smoked salmon and stirred. 'They must have thought you had something that they were desperately keen to get hold of. What more likely than the Master's confidential files?'

'Because they contain the secrets of their guilty past, you mean?'

'Yes. Why not?' She snapped off the gas and spooned the eggs and fish onto two plates.

'Eggs Rosebery,' said Bognor.

'Because of the racing colours?'

'Something like that. But what. . . .' Bognor took a plate and a glass and wandered back into the drawing-room. 'I mean, those two couldn't conceivably have guilty secrets. They were the great goody-goodies of the year. You could understand Rook or Vole or even me having something incriminating in our cupboards, but not Crutwell and Edgware.'

'But if they had, they'd want the files. Both of them up for big jobs, remember. Both relying on the Master's references. With the Master's death the files go public. Even if he was going to be nice about them while he was alive, he couldn't continue the cover-up once he was dead. Now just let's assume that they tried to steal the files from the Master's study but found someone had got there before them. Quite a chance they'd think that someone was you.'

Bognor swallowed food. It was delicious. The Clicquot too. He unbent slightly. Hermione no longer had her feet on his lap but was herself sitting upright at the other end of the long sofa. She could, he thought appreciatively, certainly scramble eggs and she *was* jolly attractive. Nevertheless . . . He made himself think of Monica. Poor old Monica all on her own at home, opening a can of baked beans for her supper. Or maybe someone would ask her out. Anyway he was far too unwell for sexual dalliance, and besides there was work to be done. 'That's solved that, then.' Bognor spoke almost flippantly. 'Edgware and Crutwell were searching for the files in my room. Heard me coming, panicked, and hit me on the head. Bastards.' Bognor said it with feeling. He still hurt like hell.

They went on eating in silence.

Then Bognor said, 'But I can't believe they killed the Master. Perhaps it was Vole.'

'Or suicide.' Hermione Frinton swallowed the last of her eggs and put her plate down on the low table.

'Mighty funny way to commit suicide,' said Bognor. He too put his plate down and leaned back, feeling more relaxed than he had for ages. He closed his eyes and sighed, then opened them in a panic to find that he was looking straight into Dr Frinton's at a range of inches.

Seconds later he was being kissed. At first he made absolutely no response, but as the kiss wore on he found that it was impossible not to be impressed and flattered by Dr Frinton's ardour, enthusiasm and vigour. It seemed churlish for him not to kiss back. Also, after a while, his pride came into it. He was damned if he was going to be outkissed by a mere English tutor, even if she was a woman. The whole exercise was so exciting that after a while breathing became quite difficult and every time he attempted to break away for air Hermione clamped her mouth even more tightly over his. He was afraid she'd break a tooth. She was also beginning to do arousing things with the rest of her body. Bells started to ring. For a while Bognor assumed the bells were in his mind, but after a while they sounded so real that he wondered if they came from outside. Evidently he was not the only one to wonder about this, because her ardour slowly diminished until she stopped kissing altogether and withdrew. She still had him pinioned securely to the sofa, but she stopped moving and lay panting lightly and listening to the insistent rings of the doorbell.

'Sugar!' she said, and attacked him again as passionately as before. The bells continued, so that she withdrew again after only about thirty seconds.

'Hadn't you better answer it?' asked Bognor, wondering if she had drawn blood. His lips felt as if they had been attacked by a ferret.

'They may go away,' she said.

For a few seconds they went on listening. Again and again the bell rang. It became obvious that the caller was not going to leave. There was a pause, then muffled shouting.

'Bloody hell!' said Hermione. She got up and went to the intercom switch which she flicked on.

Instantly the sound of an angry chief-inspector chappie filled the room. 'I know you're there. Open up. No use taking the phone off the hook. It's important! Come on! Be your age.'

Hermione turned the machine off and gazed at Bognor, anguished.

Bognor gazed back. 'He's not going to go away,' said Bognor. 'In fact I'd say he was going to break the door down in a minute.'

'Sod!' she said, brushing hair out of her eyes. 'What a sense of timing!'

'Business before pleasure.' Bognor smiled. He felt like Sir George White at the relief of Ladysmith. He smiled back at Hermione as she stood looking down at him, a passionate study in frustration.

Eventually she went back to the machine, switched it on and called down to Smith. 'Come on up,' she said shortly. 'Door's open.'

Bognor dabbed at his lips and straightened his tie.

Hermione shrugged. 'Can't win 'em all,' she said. 'I just hope there's a next time.'

Bognor was not sure what he thought about this, though he feared he might well succumb to temptation, enjoy himself hugely and then suffer fearful self-recrimination.

Such reflections were interrupted by the irruption from the nether regions of the house of the inspector himself, quivering with fury and self-importance. He took in the dishevelled appearance of his two colleagues, plus the bottle of champagne and the empty plates, grinned sourly and said he was sorry to disturb them after hours, but one or two things had come up which he wanted discussed. He had tried phoning but the phone appeared to be off the hook.

'Correct,' confirmed Hermione. 'I always take the phone off when I'm meditating. I must have forgotten to replace it. Simon came in mid-think.'

Smith said nothing but managed, with the tiniest flick of an eyebrow, to convey that gross impropriety had taken place.

'Drink?' asked Hermione, with the poise of the natural hostess. She gestured towards the half-empty bottle of Clicquot.

'Got anything a bit less arty-tarty?'

'Scotch?'

'Scotch would be perfect.'

Hermione went to fetch some.

Smith turned to Bognor. 'You seem to have made a speedy recovery,' he said sardonically. 'Wouldn't have thought of you as being a particularly fast worker. Congratulations.'

'As a matter of fact . . .' Bognor began, but was silenced by his hostess's return.

Smith accepted his drink, which looked stiff, took a sip and said, 'Right, then. Some new facts have come to light. First off, one of my men found a briefcase at the Old Bakehouse, initials "SV" for Sebastian Vole, sundry papers of no interest or importance, but an empty folder clearly indicating that it once contained the missing file from the Master's study.'

'Gosh!' said Bognor. 'So it was Vole who nicked them.'

'Vole nicked 'em and Aveline now has 'em.' The inspector licked his lips. 'A nice little bonus for the Ivans as the Cold War enters its next round.'

'Except that if Beckenham was one of theirs,' said Hermione, 'they'd know already.'

'Wouldn't be sure of that,' said the inspector. 'Can't say I begin to understand where the loyalties of that sort of person lie, but I'm inclined to think that there are people who put College before God, Queen or Country.'

'Very perceptive,' said Bognor. 'You mean Beckenham would have betrayed anything to the Russians except the good name of the college?'

'That's exactly what I mean,' said Smith. He looked at Bognor quizzically. 'You extracting the Michael?' he asked suspiciously.

'Not in the least,' said Bognor. 'I think there's much truth in what you say. But if Vole stole the files, where does that get us?'

'Can't say for sure,' said the inspector. 'That's one of the things I want to discuss. Now, another thing is your Humphrey Rook's got alibis all over the auction. Seems to have spent all relevant periods closeted with impeccable witnesses in the City of London. That doesn't mean he's innocent of the Master's murder, but it does mean he didn't break into the Randolph and clobber you.'

'I see.' Bognor poured more Clicquot for himself and Hermione.

'However.' The inspector stabbed the air with a stubby forefinger, indicating that a significant revelation was about to ensue. 'Two of our candidates are missing.'

'Missing?' said Hermione. 'This business of people

missing isn't good enough. Who now, apart from Aveline?'

'Ian Edgware and Peter Crutwell,' said Smith, eyes gleaming.

'What do you mean, "missing"?' asked Bognor. 'I saw them yesterday in a red Range Rover in the High. We were talking about it just before you arrived.'

The inspector let this blatant piece of delusion pass without comment. Instead he said, 'I called the FO and they said Edgware was on leave. When I called home his wife said he was on a special Foreign Office course.'

'Learning Urdu and unarmed combat, no doubt,' said Bognor flippantly.

'And,' continued Smith, 'when I got on to Ampleside I was told that Crutwell was away on a recce in the Western Highlands of Scotland. Something to do with the school commando camp next winter. Or the Duke of Edinburgh's Award Scheme.'

'The Duke of Edinburgh has a lot to answer for,' said Bognor with feeling. 'I suppose Crutwell is sleeping rough and living off the land miles from the nearest telephone. That would be in character.'

'That's what they told me.'

'And when's he due back?'

'They don't seem to know.'

'Honestly,' said Bognor. 'It costs £4000 a year to send a boy to Ampleside and they haven't the foggiest idea where their staff are. If I were an Ampleside parent I'd be hopping. Absolutely hopping!'

'Oh, God.' Hermione stifled a mock yawn. 'This is getting us nowhere. In fact,' and she shot both men meaningful glances, 'I've been getting nowhere all day.'

Bognor was about to expostulate, but Smith spoke first.

'I'm not at all happy with the way our investigations are proceeding,' he said. 'We started off with what could perfectly well have been passed off as a heart attack, and now we've got two murders and a major political scandal. We've got a handful of suspects who are turning out to have some surprisingly dubious sides to their characters, but we're no further on than when we started.'

'Less,' said Bognor, unnecessarily. 'Minus two, plus

nothing.'

'So what do you suggest, super-sleuths?' asked Hermione.

'Wish I knew.' The inspector looked at the end of his tether. He might not have been hit on the head, but he had been up all night and he was making a negative impression on the case. He was becoming depressed and he was exhausted.

'Do we have anything more on the stuff in the bottle? The stuff that actually killed him.'

Smith shook his head. 'Not difficult to find if you know a chemist. Our suspects would have been able to get hold of it. No problem.'

'What about finding traces of it anywhere else? Have we searched?' Hermione looked almost as depressed as her guests.'

'No sight nor sound,' said Smith. 'But I wouldn't expect it. We're dealing with educated murderers here, not your common or garden rapist or bank robber. This is intellectual stuff, and if my hunch is right, intellectuals make different sorts of mistakes to your ordinary villain.'

'But we're dealing with amateurs,' said Bognor.

'The inspector's right,' said Hermione. 'Amateurs per-haps, but educated amateurs. Apocrypha men with all the arrogance which that implies. Arrogant amateurs, my dar-lings, will make mistakes, given time.'

'Aveline wasn't an amateur,' said Smith, with respect. 'Proper pro, that one.'

Bognor yawned. 'I don't know about you lot, but I'm just about ready for bed,' he announced plaintively.

Hermione Frinton gave him a poisonous glare which made it abundantly clear that she had been ready for bed about an hour ago.

Bognor flushed. The inspector inspected the highly polished toes of his functional black shoes.

'And so where, precisely,' inquired Hermione in glacial tones, 'do we go from here?'

Bognor was on the point of saying 'back to the Randolph', but quailed and thought better of it. 'Seems to me,' he said, 'that you two should go over all the Oxford evidence, such as it is. I'd better check in with Parkinson, who's been trying to get hold of me all day. And then I shall submit Master Rook to a rigorous interrogation on the subject of his political theory paper, and allied matters.'

A certain glumness greeted this less than sensational proposal.

'All right,' he said. 'Anyone got any better ideas?'

The silence implied that no one had. Smith said he had better be getting home. He would do his best to track down Edgware and Crutwell. Hermione would go over the events of the evening with Mitten once more. All three knew that they had little better to offer than a collective Micawber. At present, and until something turned up – which, they might say, they were hourly expecting – they had nothing to do but go through motions. In the case of anything turning up (of which they were far from confident) they would go about their duties with renewed enthusiasm. But for the moment they were grave, not to say miserable.

Smith offered Bognor a lift, and he accepted. Lingering on the threshold as the inspector descended the stairs, Bognor kissed Dr Frinton chastely.

'Are you *sure* you won't stay?' she asked, running a finger down his stubbly cheek.

'I'd love to,' he said very quietly. 'But I'd be quite useless. I'm absolutely knackered. Simply couldn't cope.'

She shrugged, uncharacteristically subdued. 'Story of my life,' she said. 'Luck of the Frintons.'

'Anyway, I'm a happily married man. You shouldn't make passes at married men.'

'Don't be absurd,' she purred, a little humour coming back into her voice. 'I *only* make passes at happily married men. Single men are deathly dull and I'm incorrigible. I shan't give up, you know.'

From down below, in the area of the house reserved for the Vegan Brotherhood for International Peace and Harmony, the voice of the chief-inspector chappie came echoing up, sepulchral yet sardonic. 'Knock it off, you two,' it said. 'Remember I'm an old friend of Mrs Bognor. You've had enough trouble for one day, Bognor.'

With heavy heart and head, Bognor had to acknowledge that this was true. Slowly, he turned and went down the stairs, virtue intact, *joie de vivre* diminished, mission unfulfilled.

7

Bognor was allergic to banks. They made his palms sweat. Even when he presented a cheque for a fiver he expected the cashier to refuse it. He regarded his bank manager, a perfectly amiable Rotarian and scratch golfer, with the same apprehension as his dentist. He didn't understand money. He never had any. Yet it controlled his life and therefore, by logical extension, bankers were to be feared. They controlled his money supply which, in a materialist society, was the staff of life. Try as he might, he could not like anyone who wielded such authority over him, any more than he could bring himself, really, to like Parkinson.

These thoughts passed through his mind as he sat, sweating and twitching, in the antiseptic grandeur of the reception area at Helston's. It was a merchant bank. There was a difference, Bognor realized, between the merchant bank and the high street bank, but as far as he was concerned it was all money and therefore to be treated with caution and distrust. Helston's was a grand old bank in the Rothschild mould. The original Helston had financed the Cabots' trips to Newfoundland almost five hundred years ago, and Helston's had been juggling money ever since. Helston's, he had been told, had at least a dozen African and South American governments in their pockets. Not nice ones, either. Helston's had never been strong on scruple. A few years ago they had sold their old Victorian premises in Leadenhall Street, very close to their deadly rivals, Baring's, and moved into this glass and concrete monster in London Wall.

Bognor, arriving on time for his hastily arranged meeting with Humphrey Rook, had been given a cup of coffee and told to wait, in the nicest possible way by the nicest possible twinset-and-pearls receptionist. Nicest possible coffee too, out of the nicest possible china. He sighed, and stopped pretending to read the pink pages of the *Financial Times*. The reproduction panelling of the reception area was lined with Helstons. The artists who had painted them were no more than passing competent, but they had captured the defining family characteristic which seemed to Bognor to be greed.

It had not been a good morning. Bognor was not at his best, and he had had to catch an early train. Parkinson, he was bound to say, had been less than cordial.

'Having a crack at starting World War III single-handed, I hear,' had been his opening words. Bognor had not had the energy or even the inclination to defend himself from his superior's attacks. Instead he sat sullenly waiting for Parkinson to finish and let him get on with his job. Parkinson, he reflected as he gazed down the line of portraits opposite him, had Helston eyes: small and mean. There was no generosity in those eyes, no love, no compassion. They were not life-enhancing eyes. Bognor's eyes, though increasingly bloodshot and never especially wide open, had, he liked to think, a warmth about them. They were indicators of an open personality. Women responded to them. Parkinson's eyes were like animated marbles. His mouth wasn't up to much, either. He completely failed to understand the complexities and difficulties with which Bognor was constantly assailed. It was all very well warming a revolving civil service chair under that institutional portrait of the Queen. Naturally life looked pretty straightforward from that side of the desk, with membership of the Reform Club claimed on expenses. All Bognor got was luncheon vouchers. No doubt about it, he was simply not appreciated. It was men like him who made Britain great, while the bosses – people like Parkinson and the Helstons – got all the credit and all the loot.

'Mr Rook will see you now, Mr Bognor.' The receptionist spoke loudly and frostily, causing Bognor to suppose that she was saying the sentence for the second time.

'Good,' said Bognor, getting to his feet and dusting his trousers which had become flecked with biscuit crumbs.

'Take the lift to the seventeenth, and Mr Rook's secretary will meet you.'

'Thanks.' Bognor gave what was intended to be a haughty smile. He wanted to convey the impression that he was here to negotiate the multi-million pound financing of some ritzy petro-chemical plant and was not accustomed to being kept waiting. Alas, it was all too obvious that he was perfectly used to being kept waiting. Never mind, murder was more interesting than petro-chemicals. If the girl behind the desk knew that he was interviewing Rook about murder surely she would have been impressed. No. Bognor pursed his lips glumly. Probably not.

Alighting at the seventeenth he was greeted by another aloofly polite and immaculate secretary of the type that, on first and all subsequent impressions, confers status on the boss. It was quite clear from this girl's elegance, grooming and demeanour that Rook was earning comfortably in excess of £25,000 a year, and had the key to whatever washroom or other part of the building was at the top of the executive tree at Helston's. Hardly surprising. Apart from being such a smooth operator, Rook had married a Helston. At least Bognor thought he'd married a Helston. He'd lay long odds he had at least one steady mistress by now. Such was life.

'Simon!' exclaimed Rook unctuously, oiling out from behind a behemoth of a desk and advancing on his old Apocrypha friend with a disingenuous beam and an outstretched hand. 'I *am* sorry to have kept you. Something cropped up at the last moment. In fact between you and me Mangolo was going bankrupt and we've just had to bail her out.'

They shook hands and Rook returned to the safety of his revolving armchair.

'Mangolo?' said Bognor. 'I knew the Umdaka once.'

'George,' said Rook. 'Charming fellow. Not an enormous amount between the ears and given to extravagance. Hence his country's bankruptcy. Never mind, what's a few billion between friends? Coffee?'

'Thanks. I've just had some.'

'Ah,' said Rook. 'Good. Good. Well now . . .' He placed the tips of his fingers together and smiled. 'What can I do for you?'

Behind him loomed St Paul's Cathedral, miraculously

close. Bognor pondered the proximity of God and Mammon and wondered if Rook was given to ostentatious little excursions to mid-week communions. He wouldn't put it past him.

'This murder business,' said Bognor. 'It's about that.'

Rook made a long, lugubrious face indicating concern and *gravitas*. 'Yes,' he said. 'I imagined it was about that. Wretched business. Naturally anything I can do to help. Anything at all.'

'There's been another, I'm afraid.'

'Another?'

'Yes. Vole.'

Rook seemed genuinely surprised. 'Vole!' he exclaimed. 'You mean Seb Vole? Murdered? Whatever for? I mean, who in their right mind would want to do in a chap like Seb Vole?'

'We're almost certain it was Aveline,' said Bognor, 'but until we are absolutely certain I'd rather you didn't say anything about all this. It is rather confidential, so I'd be obliged if you'd keep it under your hat.'

'Rath*er*,' said Rook, eyes wide. 'But why Aveline? You do *mean* Aveline. Macho Max? The Regius?'

'Absolutely,' said Bognor, lowering his voice, the greater to impress the banker. He was disagreeably aware that impressing Rook was important to him. Silly, but there it was.

'But why?'

Bognor's voice dropped another few decibels so that it was only just the loud side of audible.

'This really is extremely hush-hush,' he whispered. 'It turns out that Aveline was some sort of Blunt figure, only dangerous. Really significant. The difference between being able to tell the Russians about Poussin and being able to tell them about . . . well, you know Aveline.'

'I thought I did,' said Rook. He smoothed back his already smooth sparse hair. 'But I never . . .'

'No,' conceded Bognor, 'nor me. Anyway, to cut a long story short, poor old Vole rumbled him. He was researching a *magnum opus* on moles, fifth columnists, quislings and their ilk. When he confronted Aveline with this, Aveline had him shot.'

'Good grief!' Rook *was* impressed. 'And where does

Beckenham's murder fit in with this? You mean to say Aveline had him killed, too?'

'I'm afraid I can't divulge that,' said Bognor. 'Our inquiries are still at a somewhat delicate stage.'

'But good heavens, man, it's obvious. If Aveline was going round bumping people off, then he obviously did in the Master.'

Bognor smiled tolerantly. 'I'm afraid detection's a rather more complicated and sophisticated business than that,' he said. 'No use flying by the seat of your pants in our line of country.' He was sure this was the sort of language Rook used when dealing with clients. 'The fact is,' he continued, 'we have to be alive to the possibility that the two killings were entirely, I emphasize *entirely*, unconnected.'

'Oh really!' said Rook. 'That's simply not on. College rumbles along for hundreds of years with nothing more dramatic than the occasional rustication or some idiot hurting himself climbing in late at night, then, all of a sudden there's a double murder and you say it's pure coincidence?'

'It may look peculiar, but life often does.'

Rook looked utterly incredulous.

'The fact is that we have reason to suppose that the Master may have been killed for his files.'

'For his files?'

'Or more accurately for the suppression of what was in those files.'

'Oh, yes,' said Rook slowly. 'Such as?'

Bognor chose to ignore the question, and went on, 'We recently discovered that the Master's study had been broken into and our year's files stolen.'

'Nothing to do with me,' said Rook evenly. 'I was here all the time.'

'How do you know what time I'm talking about?'

'Because I had a frankly rather impertinent call from someone called Smith. A policeman.'

'Yes,' said Bognor, 'of course. Nevertheless, I put it to you that there was material in those files which you would very much prefer to be suppressed. Particularly,' and here he injected a definite note of menace into his voice, 'in view of your involvement with the vacancy at Sheen Central.'

'What are you talking about?'

'I think you know very well what I'm talking about.' Bognor felt he should be enjoying himself more. By rights he should have the upper hand. Rook should be squirming by now, putty in his hands, ready to confess to anything. Instead he seemed surprisingly chipper, and it was Bognor who was becoming unnerved.

'Haven't a clue, old man,' said Rook. He sat back, waiting, evidently, for enlightenment.

'A little matter of your final examination papers. Political theory, to be precise. The fact that you owed your first to the pure alpha you got in political theory, and that you would never have done it if you hadn't snaffled a look at the draft paper in the Master's study weeks before the exam took place.'

'Oh,' said Rook. He smiled indulgently. 'That!'

'Yes,' said Bognor. 'That.'

'Well?'

'What do you mean "well"?' Bognor was becoming distinctly panicky now. This was not at all how he had imagined the meeting. 'That's cheating,' he blustered. 'I can't think the electors of Sheen Central would be any too happy to think they were being represented by a cheat and a liar.'

'I don't see why not,' said Rook. He smiled. 'No, seriously old man, tell me exactly what it is that you're getting at. Are you implying that I killed Beckenham?'

'Um,' said Bognor. 'Well, in a manner of speaking. That is to say, yes.'

'But you don't really believe it, do you?'

'Shouldn't I?'

'I know you're not exactly alpha material,' said Rook, 'but you're not a *complete* fool.'

Bognor said nothing.

'I suppose Molly told you,' continued Rook. 'You knew her on the *Globe* when you were dealing with that St John Derby scandal, didn't you? It's true it's not something I choose to broadcast to all and sundry, but it's a long time ago and even if old Beckenham had chosen to blurt it out to the selection committee at Sheen, which I very much doubt, I can't see it would do me any harm.'

'But it was cheating.'

'Now look, old fruit. Put yourself in my position. I have a tutorial with our much loved Master. Right? Are you following me?'

'Yes.'

'So I turn up at his study as per normal and I find he's not there. Slipped out for a slash. Right. Still with me?'

Bognor nodded.

'So I'm standing there killing time, and what do I see lying about for all to see but a political theory paper. And since political theory is what the Master and I meet to discuss every week, what could be more natural than that I should take a bit of a gander at it, eh?'

Bognor nodded. 'Go on,' he said forlornly. Rook was going to make an excellent Member of Parliament. He had the successful politician's knack of making rank dishonesty seem perfectly honourable. In a second he would be making it seem courageous, too.

'As it happens, I'd read half the questions before I realized it was our own paper and not an old one, by which time the damage was done. I didn't try to hide it, either. The Master *knew* . . . if anyone was to blame, it was him. He could have produced a new paper.'

Bognor gazed glumly over Rook's shoulder at Sir Christopher Wren's masterpiece. The trouble with Rook, or one of the troubles with Rook, was his plausibility. Impossible to know whether he was telling the truth or not. But his defence did have an awful conviction.

'Do you know if the Sheen selection committee asked the Master for a reference?'

'As it happens, they did, for the very good reason that I gave his name as a referee. What's more, I heard from him a couple of days before the gaudy, congratulating me on making the short-list and saying that if his testimonial had anything to do with it I'd win the nomination *nem. con.* And if you don't believe me I've got the letter at home. I imagine Beckenham would have kept a copy of the testimonial on file too. So, one way and another, I rather think I'm in the clear.'

'Yes,' said Bognor wearily. 'It does look like it.'

'Sorry about that.'

'What?'

'Foiling you. I do see that you want to make an arrest.' Rook stood up and paced to a bookcase covered with photographs of Helstons, children, dogs and one or two pictures of Rook shaking hands with associated Tory notables including Mrs Thatcher. As he paced he jangled the change in his trouser pocket in a manner which Bognor found profoundly irritating.

'Nothing personal,' said Bognor, lying.

'Oh, quite,' said Rook, not believing him but having already thought of a satisfactory way of levelling the score. 'But,' he paused and rubbed his jaw thoughtfully, 'I think I may be able to help you out, old boy. You see there's something I daresay you don't know and which might be relevant. Disturbingly relevant, now I come to think of it.'

He sat down again, heavily, and Bognor was struck by the fleshiness which prosperous middle age was bringing to that once gaunt-boned face.

'I expect I'm right in thinking that your prime suspects are those of us who were having a noggin with the old bean after our less than sumptuous repast on Saturday evening.'

'Just about.'

'Mitten's men, in fact.'

'Yes.'

'Not Mitten, though? Or that Frinton piece with the legs?'

'I don't think . . .' said Bognor. 'That is to say . . .'

'Do you want help, or don't you?'

'Naturally I want any help you can give me, but I can't tell you everything about our inquiries. Besides,' Bognor rallied, 'if you did have helpful information and were to withhold it then you'd be obstructing the police in the exercise of their duties.'

'Would I?'

'Indubitably.'

'Well, if you say so. It's scarcely relevant since I'm going to help you anyway, whether you like it or not.' He smiled, showing a wide expanse of gum and uneven teeth, not very white. 'You were quite young when you came up, weren't you?'

'Not especially,' said Bognor. 'I didn't do National Service or anything like that, but then none of us did.'

'I mean young for your age. Led a sheltered sort of a life. Hadn't knocked around a great deal. Not entirely clear about what was what.'

'You could say that, I suppose. It never really occurred to me.'

'No. It wouldn't, would it?'

It struck Bognor quite suddenly that Rook must have been the school bully before coming up to Oxford.

'The point I'm making,' said Rook, standing up again and jangling the change in his pocket more ferociously than ever, 'is that you may have thought one or two people were nicer than they really were.'

'I tend to think the best of people.' Bognor was painfully aware of sounding prissy.

Rook gave him another gummy smile. 'Spot on, old fruit. I, on the other hand, temper my Christian humility and love of my fellow man with a certain realism. I do happen to believe in original sin.'

Bognor hadn't the first idea of what he was driving at. However he had a shrewd enough idea of Rook's character to know that he was driving at something.

'Take Edgware and Crutwell,' said Rook.

Bognor frowned and, metaphorically speaking, took a firm grasp on both.

'Pure as the driven snow, no doubt. Butter wouldn't melt in their mouths. Eh?'

'That's putting it a bit strong,' said Bognor, 'but I never heard anything said against them.'

'Never heard about the Apocrypha choir school racket?'

'No.'

'That's what I mean, you see.' Rook looked avuncular, like a schoolmaster imparting the facts of life to a confirmation candidate. 'Well,' he said, 'I wouldn't tell you now except that circumstances demand it. I make no accusations, mind. I'm simply pointing out that people other than me have more compelling reasons for wanting those files kept secret. Now tell me, do you remember that both Crutwell and Edgware sang in the chapel choir?'

'Yes. Peter Crutwell was a bass. Ian Edgware was a tenor.'

'You never questioned it?'

'No.'

Rook looked up at the ceiling as if to say that the naivety of some people was truly staggering. 'Nothing to do with music. Nothing to do with Christianity,' said Rook. 'So what's left?'

'To judge from your expression and general manner I assume you're going to say "choirboys".'

' 'fraid so. Edgware and Crutwell were the original Bertie Wooftahs, but it wasn't just each other they were interested in. They were after the pretty little boys in the choir.'

'Crutwell and Edgware? But they're both happily married with children. As a matter of fact they both, quite independently, showed me photographs of their families the other night at the gaudy.'

'Well, there you are then.' Rook smiled his sardonic smile again. 'That ought to have aroused your suspicions. Never trust anyone who shows you snaps of their kiddiwinks at dinner. Not natural.'

Bognor glanced ostentatiously at the assorted family pictures along the top of the bookcase.

Rook fielded the reference. 'Hardly the same thing, old dear,' he said, simpering. 'But it's worse than that. You see Crutwell and Edgware realized they were onto rather a good thing with the Apocrypha choir school. Quite the sweetest little boys in town who'd do anything for a packet of crisps or a box of Smarties, or so I'm told. So our friends turned it into a commercial operation.'

'Oh, come on! Now you *are* pulling my leg.' But even as he said it, Bognor realized that Rook was being quite serious.

'I'll bet it's all on the file,' he said. 'They were running a child prostitution racket, that's what it comes down to. But there was a scandal in the end. It was inevitable. They tried to be careful, but after a while someone talked. Funnily enough, I don't believe any parent ever discovered, so old Beckenham and the choirmaster managed to hush it up.'

'How did *you* know?'

Rook smirked again. 'They weren't all that clever at telling a Wooftah from what it now pleases those who know to call "a straight". They decided I was a bit bent, and offered me the star alto for a fiver. Not my taste, so I declined.'

'And told the Master?'

'Not me,' said Rook. 'No reason to. I don't know how old Beckenham found out, but he kept his nose close to the ground. He missed less than you suppose.'

'They never propositioned me,' said Bognor, not sure whether to be proud or aggrieved.

'Naturally not. You were far too sea-green incorruptible. As I said, young for your age. Besides, you were always entwined with that big goofy thing from St Hilda's who player lacrosse.'

'LMH actually,' said Bognor peevishly. 'And netball, not lacrosse.'

'Monica something.'

'Monica Bognor, actually.' Bognor knew when to be stuffy. 'We got married.'

'Did you?' Rook looked speculative. 'Anyway, it was hardly surprising they didn't offer you choirboys when you were embroiled with a big girl like that.'

'I see.'

'What I'm getting at,' said Rook, 'is that it's one thing to have a Wooftah ambassador − they're two a penny, so it doesn't matter if Edgware likes a bit of the other. But it's scarcely going to appeal to the governors of Fraffleigh. Frankly, Crutwell's lucky to have got as far as he has in education. Housebeak at Ampleside is not to be sneezed at, but I wouldn't be happy if I were a parent of one of his boys. It's not the undermatrons he's interested in, I can tell you. My guess is that Crutwell, who's always been an ambitious little shit, would do practically anything for a headmastership.'

'Kill?' asked Bognor.

'I'd have said he was too wet,' opined Rook. 'But you can never tell with Wooftahs. We employ one or two here. Hard as nails, some of them. Bloody ruthless, I can tell you. But not Crutwell.'

'As it happens, Crutwell is at this very moment bashing around the mountains of western Scotland, sleeping rough and generally being phenomenally Spartan,' said Bognor.

'Typical Wooftah behaviour,' said Rook. 'Doesn't prove a blind thing except he's a masochist. Certainly doesn't mean he slipped a lethal dose of something in the Master's raspberry firewater. And now,' he fished out a gold watch from his waistcoat, squinted at it and went on, 'I'm afraid I'm going to have to shove you out. Henry Kissinger's lunching. Do hope I've been some help.' He stood, jangled some change, shook hands, beamed automatically. 'Tamsin will see you out,' he said. '*Very* best of luck, and if there's anything else I can possibly do to help, don't hesitate to let me know. I'm often here.'

Bognor was angry and miserable about this encounter but not nearly as angry as he was halfway through the afternoon, when, dozing at his desk, he received a phone call from Molly Mortimer of the *Globe*.

'Got you, you beast!' she shrilled. 'You owe me information. You owe me a scoop.'

'I can't give what I don't have,' he muttered.

'Don't be absurd,' said Molly. 'You and I came to a little deal over dinner before that monstrous woman in leather dragged you away.'

'Remind me.'

'A *quid pro quo*. I told you Humphrey's hidden secret, and you were going to let me have the murderer, exclusive.'

'Did I say that?' Bognor had genuinely forgotten the greater part of his Italian meal with Miss Mortimer, but now that she mentioned it the alleged deal did have a gruesome familiarity.

'You most certainly did, and I hope you're not going to try and renege.'

'I never renege,' said Bognor. 'Well, almost never. It's the family motto: "Never renege".'

'Don't be flippant with me, Simon ducky.' Bognor frowned, and tried to remember when anyone had last called him ducky. It sounded suspiciously as if Molly had been out to lunch. Still *was* out to lunch, come to that.

'So,' she said, 'are you going to tell me who did it? Or am I going to have to tell you?'

'Don't be silly,' said Bognor with asperity. 'I'm extremely busy. I'm extremely tired. I'm not at all well. I've had a distinctly tiresome meeting with your cousin Humphrey. As you so rightly surmised I'm embroiled in a complicated and intractable murder investigation and I'm not allowed to talk to the press. You'll have to go through the press office. Ask for someone called Witherspoon. Or Watherspoon. Something like that. He's your man.'

'I'm not press, I'm Molly.'

'Look, Molly, I don't want to seem brusque but I am rather tied up at the moment. I'm in the middle of a meeting and I have someone coming to see me in ten minutes and . . .' None of this was even half true, but Bognor was finding such evasions increasingly easy.

'What I'm trying to tell you, Simon dear, is that I know about Aveline.'

Bognor stopped slouching and sat very upright, spine tingling, stomach churning, head throbbing, adrenalin pumping to every extremity.

'You what?' he said, trying to keep the concern out of his voice.

'I know that Max Aveline has disappeared and that he is wanted for the murder of Lord Beckenham and a man called Vole.'

'Not true,' said Bognor. 'That is to say, "No comment."'

Inwardly he was seething. That bloody man Rook. He should never have told him. He had only done it because he wanted to impress him. Vanity, vanity. Rook's arrogant, indolent superiority had trapped him into indiscretion. He would fix him, though Heaven alone knew how.

'I hate to say this, Simon.' Suddenly Molly sounded quite sober. 'But I've spoken to the editor and we're going to lead on it tomorrow. We've done some checking already. We've found that Max Aveline has vanished, and we've found that this chap Vole's been killed, and we've learned from Vole's publishers that he was working on some espionage project, and we've got our Whitehall correspondent burrowing away. So it seems perverse of you not to tell me what's going on. Otherwise we may make mistakes. Wouldn't it be better for us to get it absolutely one hundred per cent right?'

'I can't,' he said tersely. 'You know I can't. It's more than my life's worth. Your cousin Humphrey's probably ruined me by doing this. And you won't be able to publish. We'll slap a D Notice on it.'

'We shan't pay any attention.'

'Then you and your editor will go to the Tower.'

'D Notices went out of fashion with the twist and James Bond,' snapped Molly. 'We shall publish.'

'And be damned,' said Bognor and crashed down the receiver. For several moments he stayed looking at the telephone, wondering if there was any point in ringing her back and being apologetic and conciliatory. None, he decided. Molly was doing her job. You couldn't blame her for it. She was a good journalist according to her lights, and one of a good journalist's lights was knowing how and when to betray your friends. Bognor was realist enough to know that a trustworthy journalist wasn't doing his or her job properly. But what to do?

On mature consideration and with very great reluctance indeed he acknowledged that the only course open to him was to confide in his boss. Accordingly he padded along to his office and barged in, gratified to discover him drinking tea and pondering *The Times* crossword. He looked abashed.

'You're supposed to knock, Bognor,' he said, trying to win back some initiative.

'Sorry,' said Bognor, 'I forgot. We've run into a bit of a flap.'

'Oh yes?' Parkinson regarded him steadily and expressionlessly. 'Bit of a flap, eh? Someone else shuffled off the coil as a result of your incompetence?'

'No. Nothing like that.'

'Good. Good. I'm delighted to hear it.'

'I'm afraid the press have got hold of the Aveline story.'

Parkinson picked up his pencil and bit into it. 'Got hold of the Aveline story,' he repeated.

'I'm rather afraid so, yes.'

'Held a press conference, did you? Or merely put out a release to the PA?'

'There appears to have been some sort of leak,' said Bognor, ignoring this irritatingly heavy sarcasm, 'from the Oxford end.'

'A leak from the Oxford end. I see.' Parkinson was at his most withering. 'No point in thinking it's anything to do with a sieve like you?'

Bognor flinched but said nothing.

'How do you know this?'

'I was telephoned by a reporter on the *Globe*.'

'Of course. You have these unfortunate associations with the *Globe*. You are aware that it is an offence to talk to the press. That's Witherspoon's job.'

'That's what I told them.'

Parkinson glared. 'Don't get clever with me, Bognor,' he said.

'I wasn't being clever. Absolutely not.'

'No. Silly of me.' Parkinson shut his eyes and appeared to be muttering something silently but ferociously.

'You all right?' asked Bognor.

'No,' said Parkinson opening his eyes again. 'I am not in the least all right and I am, as they say, all the worse for seeing you. I should be obliged if you would remove yourself forthwith. If I were you I should hide under the largest stone you can find. Meanwhile I shall endeavour to salvage something from the wreckage.' He shut his eyes. 'Please go!' he hissed. 'At once. And stay away.'

Bognor, for once, did as he was told.

Back in his office he discovered that Inspector Smith had telephoned and left a message. The girl on the switchboard who had taken it said succinctly, 'A Mr Smith rang and said that a Mr Crutwell was back at home now and Mr Edgware with him.'

'That all?' he asked.

'Yes,' said the girl. 'He seemed to think you'd understand.'

Bognor sighed. No point in hanging around the office and possibly being seen by Parkinson. It was a good excuse for getting away. He had little hope of a meeting with the two men yielding anything of interest. In view of Rook's appalling treachery he was disinclined to believe his story of the Apocrypha choir school racket, which was almost certainly a malicious red herring designed to create bad blood between Bognor and Crutwell and Edgware and deflect attention from Rook. Nevertheless it would have to be checked, unpalatable though the checking would undoubtedly be. He wondered whether to arrange an appointment or simply turn up, whether to drive or go by train. Decisions, decisions, he thought desperately, and decided to toss a coin. His mind was not up to freedom of choice. In the event he set off by train, unannounced.

Ampleside was not a major public school and yet to call it a minor public school was less than fair. It hovered in a sort of no man's land between the excellent and the mediocre, never quite sure whether it was on the verge of promotion from the second division or relegation from the first. If you accepted Evelyn Waugh's grades ('leading school, first-rate school, good school and school'), then Ampleside was either among the last of the leading or the first of the first-rate. But Waugh's caveat about these definitions should be remembered ('Frankly,' said Mr Levy, '"school" is pretty bad'). Ampleside was not bad, not bad at all, but it seldom attained excellence or even aspired to it. It was worthy, it was hardworking, it was hearty and it was dull.

Reaching Ampleside Station shortly after six, Bognor, who had never previously visited the place, learned that the school and its constituent houses were on the outskirts of town, some fifteen minutes' walk away. It was a fine evening and, despite the continuing fragility of his condition, Bognor had no objection to hoofing it. The exercise might clear the brain. In any case walking was the next best thing to jogging; if he walked often and fast enough he might one day build up to a gentle jog. It was unlikely but possible.

The town was quiet, pleasant without being picturesque, and just too small to be disfigured by an excrescence of large chain stores and supermarkets. In the wide main street, with a number of battered half-timbered houses, Bognor noticed a couple of almost serious bookshops and one or two pubs which looked like serious drinking places. He was tempted to drop in for a pint but thought better of it. Time for that on his return, always provided he was successful.

The school itself was less attractive than the town, being a Victorian foundation with twentieth-century additions. This meant an imposing bogus baronial front with a high tower over a gateway which was a weak parody of Apocrypha Great Gate. Also glass and concrete science blocks. It had space, however, much of it green and well mown, and peopled in places with boys in white playing out the last overs of the afternoon's cricket. Under the arch was a porter's lodge, and here Bognor stopped to inquire the whereabouts of Mr Crutwell.

'Who?' asked the school custos, a scarlet-faced pensioner of vaguely military mien.

'Crutwell,' said Bognor. 'Mr Crutwell. He's a house-master.'

The custos shook his head in evident perplexity. 'Who do you say?' he asked again.

Bognor felt the panic rising like sap. It was Ampleside that Crutwell taught at, surely? Or had he misheard or misunder-stood? Could it have been Ardingly or Alleyns or Allhallows or Abingdon or Aldenham or even Ample*forth*?

'Crutwell,' he said again. 'Mr Crutwell. C-R-U-T-W-E-L-L. Crutwell.'

The custos stared as blankly as before, and then suddenly his face became suffused with understanding. 'You mean Mr Crutwell,' he said, smiling broadly at Bognor as if *he* was the fool.

Bognor was on the point of expostulating, but realized it would only complicate matters. 'Crutwell,' he said, smiling. 'That's the chap.'

'He's housemaster of Bassingthwaite,' said the custos.

'Is he? And where's that?'

The porter grumbled to his feet, holding his back like a rheumatic in a Will Hay comedy, and staggered out into the evening's shadows. Much pointing, gesticulating and unin-telligible direction-finding ensued.

'Fine,' said Bognor. 'Thanks very much. I'm sure I'll find it quite all right.' He set off into the sunset, blinking slightly and resolved to ask the first sane boy he saw where Bassing-thwaite really was. From behind came a shout. It was the custos. Swearing silently, Bognor retraced his steps.

'You looking for Mr Crutwell?'

'That was the general sort of idea, yes.'

'You won't find him at Bassingthwaite.'

'Oh. Just as well you caught me. I might have had a wasted journey. Where will he be?'

'At Big Field watching Potters.'

'Of course,' said Bognor. 'Silly of me. I should have known. Big Field, watching Potters. Right, then. I suppose that's Big Field over there?' He pointed towards the grandest of the cricket pitches, the only one with spectators.

The custos nodded.

'Well, thank you so much. I'm much indebted to you.' And once more Bognor strode off past the ivy-covered red brick, through the lengthening shadows, across a gravelled quadrangle, through a post-war cloister complete with war memorial to Ampleside's glorious dead, and out on to Big Field. Most of the onlookers were on the far side of the ground, boys standing or sprawling on the grass, masters and their wives in canvas deckchairs. Near to him, however, a small, spotty boy was leaning against a wall, hands in pockets. At Bognor's approach he took his hands out of his pockets and stood to attention. Then, seeing that Bognor was not a member of staff, he put his hands back in his pockets and slumped against the wall.

'Is this Big Field?' asked Bognor, feeling fatuous.

The small boy gave him a look of withering contempt. Bognor withered and tried again: 'What's the score?'

'Bassingthwaite need another ten.'

Bognor looked at the scoreboard and saw that Bassingthwaite were a hundred and sixty-two for the loss of nine wickets.

'And the last pair in?'

'But one of them's Hodgkiss Major,' said the boy.

'Good is he, Hodgkiss?'

'Made a hundred against Fraffleigh,' said the boy.

Even as they spoke one of the batsmen leaned into his stroke and played what the professional commentators always call a 'cultured' cover drive for four. Amid the ripple of clapping that greeted this shot Bognor heard a familiar voice call out, 'Oh, well played, Hodgkiss!'

Following the direction of the shout, Bognor saw Peter Crutwell. Bassingthwaite's housebeak was sprawled in a deckchair whose stripes were no more alarmingly vivid than those of the blazer that covered his upper half. On his head he wore a creamy panama hat with, though Bognor found this surprising since the society's sporting affiliations and interests were non-existent, an Arkwright and Blennerhasset ribbon tied round it. Beside him, also in white flannels but hatless and with a more subdued blazer, was Ian Edgware. Both men had pipes clutched in their fists. They looked indeed as if they might have been advertising pipe tobacco, so resolutely masculine, conservative, traditional and British did they appear. Bognor remembered Rook's remarks about 'Bertie Wooftahs' and found them hard to credit now that he was on Big Field watching Potters. Murder, homosexuality, Russian agents and all the unsavoury shenanigans of the last few days seemed to belong to another, bloodier, world. Yet, if Rook was to be believed, these were the very men who had turned the Apocrypha choir school into a prostitution racket.

'Oh well,' sighed Bognor, 'only one way to find out.' And he began to walk slowly round the boundary rope in the direction of the spectators. As he walked, play, of course, progressed. The Bassingthwaite boys were moving as circumspectly as Bognor himself. Occasionally Bognor stopped to watch as the runs accumulated in a trickle, each one greeted with handclaps and a shout from Crutwell. Bognor hoped his interest in Hodgkiss Major did not go beyond the bounds of cricket.

Bognor and Bassingthwaite kept in remarkably good step, so that just as he arrived within a few yards of Crutwell's deckchair, Hodgkiss Major's bat described a slicing arc and the ball came off it square, in the rough direction of gully. It was not quite what he had intended, but it would do. Immediately Crutwell was on his feet, his pipe stuffed in his blazer pocket and his hands beating each other in heavy, rhythmical strokes as he led a very English housemaster's chorus. 'Well played, you two. *Jolly* well played. Good show, Hodgkiss. You too, Lorimer. Well played, all of you. Jolly well done, Bassingthwaite. Thoroughly good team effort. Jolly fine all-round show.' All this interspersed with the rhythmic clap of the hands, a sort of marking time. Edgware, standing at his friend's shoulder, was rather more subdued. He merely clapped, pipe rammed between his teeth and smoking slightly. He had an expression of quiet approval on his manly features. Bognor, so caught up in the occasion that he found himself clapping too, walked slowly up to them and insinuated himself in the middle.

'Good show,' said Bognor. 'Smashing finish.'

'*Jolly* good show,' echoed Edgware, somehow getting the words coherently through clenched lips and round his pipe.

'*Bloody* fine show,' said Crutwell. 'First time Bassingthwaite's won Potters since Fothergill's time.'

And then, still clapping, Crutwell and Edgware turned to look at the man in the middle, this third spectator who had just joined them. Bognor grinned at them both in turn, pleased at their sudden discomfiture.

'I really enjoyed that,' said Bognor, still clapping. 'Unexpected bonus. Who'd have thought I'd have caught the dying moment of Potters on my first-ever visit to Ampleside?'

'Oh,' said Crutwell. 'It's you.'

'Hello,' said Edgware, removing the pipe from his teeth and smiling nervously. 'What brings you to Ampleside?'

'Ah!' said Bognor. 'Well, that's a long and complicated story. I'm going to have to tell it, though. Do you have a moment?'

'Well,' Crutwell frowned. 'The chaps are going off for high tea now, and then there's prep. I suppose I can give you until prayers.'

'Which are when?'

'Nine.'

'That should be fine,' said Bognor, thinking that he could in that case take in a swift pint at one of the attractive Ampleside pubs before getting a late train home. It seemed an age since he had seen Monica, he reflected. In fact it would be distinctly agreeable to be able to put his feet up and enjoy a few hours of undisturbed peace and quiet.

'You're free, Ian?' Crutwell asked Edgware, and Edgware nodded. 'If you'll excuse me a sec while I have a quick word with my chaps, I'll be with you in half a mo,' he continued, and walked off jauntily to give his victorious team a fatherly, personal, man-to-man shake of the hand, pat on the back, and general all-round housemaster's approbation.

'Funny seeing Peter in his natural habitat,' said Edgware quietly. 'He lives for his boys.'

'Yes,' agreed Bognor, watching this latter-day Mr Chips doing his stuff. 'He's obviously very good at it.'

'Oh yes,' said Edgware. 'He'll go right to the top. The very top. Barring accidents.'

'Barring accidents,' repeated Bognor.

'I do hope,' said Edgware, fixing Bognor with an unblinking and most meaningful stare, 'that there aren't going to be any accidents.'

'I hope not, too,' said Bognor.

'I always think Apocrypha is a wonderful sort of freemasonry. Wherever you go, wherever you are, there's always an Apocrypha man to help you out.'

'Not in the Board of Trade, I'm afraid,' said Bognor. 'I'm the only Apocrypha man there. Certainly the only one in Special Operations.'

'No, I suppose not.' Edgware smiled weakly.

'But I do see,' countered Bognor, 'that in a place like the Foreign Office the Apocrypha Mafia may count for rather more.'

'I wouldn't call it a Mafia,' said Edgware.

'Oh,' said Bognor, coldly, 'wouldn't you?'

Before this exchange could become any more frigid they were rejoined by Peter Crutwell, who was rubbing his hands together and oozing euphoria from every pore.

'Tell you what,' he said. 'Why don't we take a shufti across Sneath's Meadow and see if there's a crowd at the Duck and Drake? I think this calls for a pint of shandy.'

Bognor was not going to drink shandy, but provided he could have bitter he was perfectly happy to fall in with this. A crowd, on the other hand, could be embarrassing. This was not the sort of conversation which anyone would want overheard.

'Well,' said Crutwell as they began to pace slowly towards the pub, 'what exactly does bring you here? I can't believe it's simply the magic appeal of Potters.'

'No,' said Bognor. 'I've come about the murder.'

'I see.' Crutwell put on a solemn, almost melancholy, face which Bognor guessed he used for lecturing boys prior to beating them. If beating boys was allowed still.

'What about the murder, exactly?'

'You must realize that everyone who was drinking with the Master that night is a suspect?'

'Including you?'

'Including me.'

They were approaching a river lined with willows, recently pollarded. Cows grazed on the further bank. A wooden footbridge spanned the stream which flowed fast enough to create little swirling patterns on the surface, eddies among the reeds. A couple, entwined, were strolling towards them. It was very quiet, very pastoral, very English.

'You sure he was murdered?' asked Edgware. 'Seems awfully melodramatic.'

'Quite sure,' said Bognor. 'As for melodrama – yes, I'm afraid things have been rather melodramatic lately. Sebastian Vole's been killed and Max Aveline almost certainly did it. He's fled to Russia. He's a sort of supercharged Philby, it seems. But you'll read all about that in tomorrow's papers. Even *I* was attacked.'

'I thought you looked a bit seedy,' said Edgware sympathetically. 'What happened?'

'Someone ambushed me at the Randolph.'

'Ah!'

They crossed the bridge. No one spoke. Bognor noticed a pair of ducks diving for food, bottoms waggling absurdly in the air every time they submerged themselves. Crutwell turned left, hands deep in pockets, head slumped forward, evidently deep in thought.

'Where've you been, by the way?' asked Bognor. 'I could have sworn I saw you in the High the other day. Either of you have a scarlet Range Rover?'

'Yes,' said Crutwell. 'I take it on digs. Actually it nominally belongs to the school archaeological society, but it's licensed in my name.'

'Was it you?'

'No,' said Crutwell.

'Yes,' said Edgware.

Another, longer, silence ensued, more pregnant this time. Ahead of them Bognor could see a thatched, whitewashed building with an inn sign outside as well as a scattering of picnic tables, all but one unoccupied.

Crutwell relit his pipe, an elaborate process which had the intended effect of making speech impossible. He obviously did not know what to say next, and lighting his pipe was an attempt to disguise the fact. It fooled no one, not even him.

Bognor, on the other hand, had no intention of making life easier for either of them by asking a direct question. Not yet.

'Quite empty,' said Edgware, indicating the pub.

They continued in silence.

Eventually, on reaching the garden, Bognor asked the others what they were drinking. Crutwell stayed with his shandy. Edgware, on the other hand, asked if Bognor would mind awfully if he were to have a gin and tonic. It was, he supposed, silly of him to give them the chance to get their act together while he fetched the drinks, but he had a hunch which told him that despite some evidence to the contrary it would be Edgware who would prevail. Edgware wanted to tell the truth, Crutwell to conceal it. Bognor felt confident that by the time he settled himself down in the garden the others would have decided that small lies would lead to greater ones and ultimately disaster. Crutwell, used to getting away with deceptions in a world in which his word was accepted without question, was less of a realist than Edgware, whose life was founded largely on determining the extent of deception permissible in oneself and the degree of deception being attempted by others.

Returning to their table with the drinks balanced on a battered old tin tray, Bognor found that, as he had expected, an earnest confabulation had taken the place of the earlier silences, though quiet descended again at his approach.

'Cheers,' he said, sitting down. The pub was a free house and sold draught Young's, his favourite beer. Life was looking up.

'Cheers.' The two other Apocrypha men were not going to forgo social niceties at a time like this.

'Look,' said Edgware, carefully removing the slice of lemon from his glass and depositing it on the tray, 'I'm afraid there are one or two things we have to tell you.'

'Yes,' said Bognor. He smiled, and wiped froth from his upper lip.

'The fact is,' said Edgware, 'that it *was* us you saw in the High that afternoon.'

'Yes,' said Bognor again, still smiling.

'We had rather hoped,' went on Edgware, 'that we wouldn't bump into anyone we knew.'

'I see,' said Bognor.

'The reason being,' said Crutwell, 'that we were contemplating something which wouldn't have looked very good had we been found out.'

'Theft,' said Bognor.

'Well,' Crutwell was looking very much as if he would have preferred something stronger than shandy, 'I wouldn't put it quite like that.'

'How would you put it, then?'

'Simon's quite right,' said Edgware. 'No point in pretending otherwise. We'd come up to Oxford to steal something.'

'Files from the Master's office.'

'Yes.'

'But when you got there,' said Bognor helpfully, 'you found that someone had been there before you.'

'Yes.'

'Would you mind,' asked Bognor, gently, for vestiges of affection and respect for his college, its good name, its former members and general *esprit de corps* still remained in him, 'telling me why you were so keen to get those files that you were actually prepared to nick them?'

'I imagine you know that by now,' said Crutwell, aggressively.

'I want you to tell me,' said Bognor.

'Either he knows or he doesn't know,' said Crutwell to Edgware. 'I'm damned if I see why we should make his job any easier, let alone incriminate ourselves unnecessarily.'

Edgware paid no immediate attention. 'Presumably you've read the files?'

'What makes you say that?'

'Well.' Edgware shrugged. 'It's ridiculous to suggest otherwise.'

'Suppose I were to tell you I hadn't got the files?'

'We wouldn't believe you.'

'I haven't got the files.'

'I *don't* believe you,' said Edgware angrily. 'Stop playing around, please. You're not making this easy.'

'I don't want to make it easy,' snapped Bognor. 'You didn't think about that when you hit me at the Randolph. You could have bloody killed me.'

'It was Peter,' said Edgware. 'He panicked.'

'I'm having a Scotch,' said Crutwell suddenly. 'Anybody else?'

Edgware asked for another gin, Bognor another pint.

'Leaving aside the whereabouts of the files,' said Bognor, as Crutwell disappeared towards the bar, 'you went to my room because you assumed I'd got them.'

'Yes,' said Edgware. 'We had a long talk about it. In the end it did at least seem worth a try. But I assume the police had them.'

'No. As it happens, Vole had them.'

'Vole?'

'Presumably he took them to further his researches. We'll never know. He made an awful mess of the Master's study. I should have thought that would have told you that it wasn't me. We would have been slightly more professional. You too, come to that. Don't they teach breaking and entering at the FO?'

Edgware smiled stiffly. 'Yes, but not in the public schools. Peter's admirable in most respects, but he'll never make a burglar.'

'Hmmm. Nor a headmaster, now.'

'What do you mean?'

Bognor raised his eyebrows. As he did, Crutwell emerged from the door of the pub carrying his round of drinks. He looked, in his gaudy cricket outfit, like the twelfth man carrying refreshment out to the players. Perhaps, thought Bognor, that's exactly what he's doing. Perhaps life is just a game of cricket. In which case both Edgware and Crutwell had thrown away their wickets at a crucial stage in their innings, just when they looked set for a century apiece. Silly. Careless.

Bognor took a large mouthful, suppressed a belch and decided to come briskly to the point.

'The files are in Moscow,' he said, 'with Aveline. Which means that your guilty secret can hardly be said to be safe. Now it's perfectly plain that both of you are in grave trouble, but I'm not sure that you realize how grave. It's not just a matter of your careers, your marriages, your reputations and all that. It's a matter of murder.' He paused to see if he was having the hoped-for effect. On balance, to judge from their chastened expressions, he was. 'Would it make it easier for you if I said that although I have not yet, and I emphasize "yet", had a chance to examine the files myself, I have been given an account of the business of you two and the College choir school? I don't want to indulge in any gratuitous muck-raking. I just need to confirm that, broadly speaking, it's true.'

He looked from one to the other. Neither spoke. Both nodded.

'OK,' he said. 'Ian was awaiting preferment at the FO, and Peter was hoping to get the headmastership of Fraffleigh. And you thought Beckenham would ruin your chances. Correct?'

'No,' said Edgware with vehemence, 'it's very much not it. The point is that as long as Beckenham was around we knew he wouldn't shop us. It was a long time ago, it was deeply shocking and all that, but it's over, it's in the past. Beckenham accepted that. If he'd died naturally, with some sort of warning, he would presumably have destroyed any records that incriminated us. I would think he'd destroy the files when he finished being Master. But that's just speculation. Peter and I had a shrewd idea that the files contained trouble as far as we were concerned, and we were desperately worried in case they fell into the wrong hands.'

'I see.' Bognor was suddenly depressed. Another failure loomed.

'You admit,' he said, 'that you came back to Oxford, broke into the Master's lodgings, and then into my room at the Randolph where you attacked me?'

'I really am sorry about that, old man,' said Crutwell. 'Lost my nerve.'

Bognor grimaced ruefully. 'But you deny having killed the Master?'

'I grant you,' said Edgware, 'that from a circumstantial point of view we may have to be included on your list of suspects. But as I've tried to point out, we have no motive. Lord Beckenham always played straight with us. He'd given us references before and they'd always been glowing. There was no reason to think that they wouldn't go on being glowing.'

'Even,' said Bognor, 'when the jobs were as significant as the ones you're up for? I mean, he may have been prepared to countenance the idea of having you in positions of middling power and influence, but to connive at someone with that sort of skeleton in their past getting the headmastership of Fraffleigh . . . well, surely he'd have drawn the line somewhere? I mean . . .' He gulped beer. Words failed him. The sun was going down, in more ways than one.

'I think,' said Crutwell, seeming to regain a modicum of self-confidence, 'that the Master had more, how shall I put it, *vision* . . . yes, I think that's the word, more *vision* than you credit him with. If he believed, as I think he did, that I was suitable to be headmaster of one of our great English public schools, then I don't think he'd dredge up some peccadillo from the past in order to prevent it. And the same applies to Ian. The Master clearly thought Ian should go to the very top, and that the country would frankly be damned lucky to be represented by a man of Ian's outstanding intellect and character. Why should he suddenly throw all that into jeopardy? It simply doesn't make sense. Beckenham was a great man in his way, and like a lot of great men he saw beyond detail. The little things of life didn't mean anything. He was interested in big things, Simon. He had big ideas, big hopes. He wanted to transform the world, and we were to be his instruments. He was like Milner. He nurtured his protégés because he believed in them. He believed in us. He believed in our contribution to the future. We made a mistake, a bad mistake, but he forgave us and he set it aside, because he was a big man.'

Bognor decided he was going mad. There was no alternative. 'Forgive me,' he said, incredulously, 'but did you say "peccadillo"?'

'We were very young, Simon.' Edgware at least had the diplomat's concern to appear reasonable at all times. 'Of course what we did was reprehensible, but what Peter is really saying is that the Master made his own judgements about people, and once he'd made them he stuck with them. He was very consistent and very loyal, and we repaid that loyalty and that consistency.'

Bognor could take no more. 'I used to think,' he said, voice trembling but still just controlled, 'that I quite liked old Beckenham. I knew he didn't rate me very highly, but he didn't seem to dislike me actively and he was always polite. I knew he thought Rook and you two were the great white hopes of our generation, and because I was absurdly naïve I suppose I went along with that. Now it turns out that Rook was a liar and a cheat and that you two were venal pederasts of the most revolting sort imaginable. And that he knew all along. You were all as bad as each other.' He got to his feet. 'All right,' he said. 'So you didn't kill him. Frankly I begin to wish you had. But just because I can't pin that on you, don't think you're going to get away with this. I'm not totally without influence and I promise you that I shall do everything – everything – in my power to ensure that the pair of you languish in the obscurity you so richly deserve.'

Still quivering with rage and lost illusion, he lunged off into the twilight. Behind him he left the housemaster and the diplomat contemplating each other in amazement that such innocence and altruism could still stalk the land, even though it was confined to the lower regions of the Board of Trade.

8

It was a relief to be home with Monica. Gadding about was all very well for a time and in its way, but Bognor was essentially a lethargic animal dedicated to creature comforts. His most besetting sin was sloth, and what he really liked was warmth, security, predictability and a quiet life. There were moments when he wished he were a gayer (in the true sense) blade, but he knew that he was not cut out for it. True, he lusted in a wistful way after leggy ladies like Dr Frinton, but when it came to the point he tended to find them more alarming than alluring and he would be disconcerted to wake up with a strange face beside him every morning. Monica was putting on weight. The line of her jaw was not as firm as it once was, but then no one could accuse *him* of being an oil painting. He had never been more than a watercolour, even in his prime, and he was now firmly in the lithograph class – in an unlimited edition, too. Still, for all his faults he was basically nice in the same sort of way that Rook, Crutwell and Edgware were deep down nasty. Monica was nice, too. Both had a considerable capacity for naughtiness but not, he liked to think, for evil. They were capable of infinite sorts of over-indulgence, but never of malice. They were well suited to each other and fitted each other like old gloves, though it did them good to get away from each other occasionally, if only because the reunions were so agreeable.

It was with thoughts such as these racketing around his mind that he let himself into the flat after the upsetting trip to Ampleside. Monica was in bed reading *Phineas Redux*.

'Hello, you,' she said. 'Have you eaten?'

'Had a pork pie on the train,' he said. He had eaten two Mars bars, too, but thought it better not to admit to them.

They kissed. 'Missed you,' he said.

'Me too.'

They kissed again.

'You don't look too hot,' she said, pushing him away to get a sense of perspective on him.

'I'm not too hot,' he said, 'as a matter of fact. Tell you what, why don't I make us both a mug of chocolate and tell you all about it?'

'With marshmallow.'

'All right.'

In the end it was she, taking pity on his fragile and battered appearance, who made the chocolate while he changed into his striped pyjamas. Then they both clambered into bed and sat up drinking chocolate while Bognor told his story.

'Aveline?' asked Monica when he got to the Regius Professor. 'Did you say Aveline?'

'Yes.'

'Professor Max Aveline?'

'Yes. Why?'

'Because he just called. It was a terrible line. Sounded as if he was in Siberia.'

'He probably was. Are you sure it was Aveline?'

'Almost. It was a really rotten line, but I'm virtually certain he said his name was Professor Max Aveline.'

Bognor stared at the frothy marshmallow on top of his drink. 'I think I may be about to become lucky,' he said, kissing the tip of his wife's nose. 'What did he say?'

'Wanted to know when you'd be home, and said he'd ring back later. Sounded rather over-excited.'

'I daresay he did,' said Bognor. 'It's catching, too. I think I'm about to become over-excited myself.'

'Explain,' said Monica. 'You haven't finished.'

Fifteen minutes later, having included everything except one or two details concerning Molly Mortimer and Hermione Frinton, he said, 'So that's it.'

'Quite a story,' she said, snuggling up to him. 'Let me look.' She peered into his hair like a mother monkey inspecting for fleas.

'Ouch!' she exclaimed. 'Nasty.'

'Thanks,' he said. 'Some people have been inclined to laugh at my wounds and make out that three stitches are a trivial matter.'

'Not me. Looks horrid.'

'For once I agree with Rook. They are a pair of extremely disagreeable Bertie Wooftahs and I intend sorting them out.'

'You do just that.' She giggled.

'What time did Aveline say he'd phone again?'

'He didn't. I just told him you'd be in before midnight.'

Bognor glanced at his watch, and even as he did the phone shrilled. He picked it up at once. 'Bognor,' he snapped in his most official manner. Static, crackling, clicks and alien tongues assaulted his ears. Bognor put his hand over the mouthpiece. 'I think he's lost his roubles,' he said. He removed his hand and addressed himself to the phone. 'Hello!' he called. 'Hello! Hello! Hello! Moscow, can you hear me?'

Down the line a woman's voice answered him back. 'London! London! Hello, London, can you hear me? This is Moscow calling.' The voice faded and was replaced by more breakfast cereal noises, then just as Bognor was about to put the machine down in despair the line became miraculously cleared and the donnishly English voice of the Regius Professor of Sociology was saying 'Bognor . . . Bognor . . . is that you? God, the bloody phones in this bloody country are worse than the bloody phones in bloody England.'

'Yes,' said Bognor. 'Hello. Yes, it's me. Bognor here. Bognor speaking.'

'Can you hear me? It's three o'clock in the bloody morning here.'

'It's midnight here.'

'I didn't phone to discuss the time. What's this about my having murdered Beckenham?'

'What?'

'It's a very bad line.' Aveline was shouting. 'I can't hear you. What?'

'I don't know anything about your having murdered Beckenham,' said Bognor. 'I assume you had poor Sebastian Vole done away with, but I know nothing about your having killed Beckenham. Did you?'

157

'That's what I'm ringing to tell you. It's unfortunate about Vole. We had no alternative. He'd been very conscientious and surprisingly astute, but that's by the way. I wish to make it absolutely plain that I did not kill Beckenham. He was a valued colleague. To say that I killed him is the grossest calumny.'

Bognor didn't think it possible to calumnize a former Regius Professor who turned out to be a traitor and a murderer.

'How do you know all this, anyway?' asked Bognor.

'I'm told by my friends that the *Daily Globe* is publishing a story tomorrow. I assumed it was a leak inspired by you and your friend Dr Frinton.'

'Far from it.'

There was a snort of disbelief from the Moscow end. 'I do not propose to be a scapegoat for your incompetence.'

'All right,' Bognor bridled. 'If you didn't do it, then who the hell did?'

'I wouldn't expect you to believe me,' said Aveline. 'However, a colleague of mine will be in touch with you as soon as possible. I spoke to him earlier this evening. It was he who tipped me off. He'll tell you who Beckenham's murderer was. I can't identify him beyond saying that he will call himself "Q". He is a senior officer of British Intelligence, but you won't know him. I think you'll believe him, though. You'll find he knows more about you than you yourself. That's all. He'll be in touch. Goodnight.'

Bognor stared at the receiver with disbelief. 'Would you believe it?' he said eventually. 'That bastard Aveline is trying to clear his name.'

'How do you mean?' asked Monica. 'If he's in Moscow he can hardly deny being one of theirs.'

'No, not that,' said Bognor. 'He's not the least bit ashamed of that. Nor of having old Vole killed. But he doesn't want it to be thought he killed the Master.'

'And did he?'

'God knows.' He finished the dregs of his now rather cold chocolate and put the mug on the bedside table. 'Someone called "Q" is going to be in touch.'

'"Q"?' Monica giggled. 'Who's he?'

'Something in Intelligence. Our Intelligence. Theirs too, I presume. A triple agent at least.'

He turned out the light. 'If you want my opinion,' he said, 'there's no intelligent life in Intelligence.'

'Ha bloody ha,' she scoffed.

He silenced her with a kiss.

'Ugh,' she said, struggling free. 'You reek of chocolate.'

Next morning there was a note on the doormat along with a final demand from the Gas Board and a circular from a mail order firm offering life-size reproductions of sculpture by Moore, Hepworth and Elizabeth Frink made from reinforced papier mâché. The note, produced on a manual typewriter, read: 'Round Pond. 11. Will be wearing A and B tie. Q.'

'Can't get more cryptic than that,' said Bognor, showing it to Monica.

She read it three times, held it up to the light, and finally said, 'Oh, do be careful, Simon.'

'Careful? How do you mean, careful?'

'I mean don't get shot or abducted.'

'In Kensington Gardens? Be your age.'

'I am. The Iranian Embassy's only just down the road. If this man really is a triple agent there's no telling what he may get up to. There are corpses all over the place in this case, Simon, so for heaven's sake be careful.'

'If anything awful happens I'll scream blue murder and hordes of hirsute Norland nannies will attack the hapless "Q" with raised umbrellas. Led by Wendy Craig, no doubt.'

'Now you're being ridiculous.'

'Not in the least. I feel in the mood for toast. If I'm going to be shot by this anonymous figure in Arkwright and Blenner-hasset neckwear I might as well eat a hearty breakfast.'

'I do wish you wouldn't be frivolous.' Monica sighed and went to percolate coffee and titivate.

An hour or so later Bognor sauntered up Kensington High Street past the Royal Garden Hotel and through the gates of the gardens. It was hot. One or two au pairs, not all nubile, sunned themselves on the grass in bikinis. Men in abbreviated bathing trunks with oily olive skins and muscles disported themselves similarly. Waiters, thought Bognor, pulling his stomach in and trying to appear jaunty. He smiled cheekily

at a big-busted blonde in an emerald-green job which reminded him of Hermione Frinton's All Souls' leotard, and
was upset when she turned away contemptuously. He really
must be getting old.

At the pond there was the usual gaggle of exceedingly rich
infants in superannuated perambulators attended by nurse-
maids and nannies in starched uniforms. Older children and
pensioners played with boats, many of them remote-con-
trolled. And on one of the benches, reading a copy of *Horse
and Hound* magazine, sat a small grey man in a pink and
purple tie.

'So that's "Q",' thought Bognor. He was very small,
rather neat, quite unrecognizable. The sort of man who
merged. He would never be noticeable, never be out of place.
As Bognor contemplated him from afar, he looked up and
smiled. It was an oddly attractive smile. Bognor had not
anticipated meeting a likeable man, and yet he felt an unexpected warmth from him. He could have been any age over
sixty, white-haired, heavily lined, but amused in appearance
and, Bognor thought, probably amusing too.

He folded the magazine and placed it alongside him on the
park bench, then looked up again and smiled. Bognor
noticed for the first time that he had a little silvery goatee
beard. He did not move. Bognor was obviously supposed to
go to him. He did.

'Morning, Simon,' said the man, very nonchalantly, as if
this meeting was a pleasant, unremarkable coincidence and
Bognor an old friend. 'Pray sit.'

Bognor sat.

'I was sorry,' said 'Q', 'to hear about your mother's cat.'

Bognor winced. His mother's cat had been run over a
fortnight before in Letchworth. Hardly anyone knew he had
a mother, not even Parkinson. And scarcely one of those who
knew he had a mother knew the mother had a cat.

'It was quite an old cat,' said Bognor. 'Smelly, too. Can't
say I cared for it.'

'Your application for transfer, by the way . . .' The little
man shook his head. 'You're far too valuable where you are,
you know. I fear you're there for life, whatever Parkinson
may think.'

'Look,' said Bognor. 'Who are you? And who . . . and why . . . and are you entitled to wear that tie?' It was an odd question to ask, but there was something un-Apocryphal about him which was disturbing.

'Just call me "Q",' he said. 'Better that way. And since you ask, I suppose I'm not strictly speaking entitled to the tie. No. Does it matter?'

Bognor said he supposed not. The man laughed at this. He had a cane which he picked up and used to beat the tarmac with. It was wooden, ash perhaps, with a silver handle. Could have been a swordstick. 'Q' could have been a fencer. He had an agile air.

'Well,' he said. 'I'll be brief. Are you ready to believe?'

'I'm not sure,' said Bognor. 'I don't care for this secrecy. I don't like to believe what I hear from a man with no name. Do you have any proof of identity? A card? A letter? Can't I know more? Whose side are you on? Ours or theirs?'

'Q' seemed to consider this very seriously for a minute or two, and then he said solemnly, 'I don't think I can answer that. You see, at my level of Intelligence work the question ceases to have meaning. I work to please myself. I have no other master. Contacts, friends, allegiances, alliances. . . . But sides? I prefer not to take sides.'

'I see.' Bognor was perplexed. At the same time he knew a cul-de-sac when he saw one. 'OK,' he said. 'You have a message for me and I'm disposed to believe it. I have precious little alternative. Go ahead and tell me.'

'You realize Aveline's defection is a national scandal?'

Bognor had read the *Globe*, seen the breakfast news and heard Peter Jay's homily. 'I suppose,' he said.

'I have no particular brief for Aveline,' said 'Q', 'though he'll be much maligned, and he has an honesty of sorts. For myself, I like to see records as straight as possible, so I tell you this and leave you to decide what to do with the information. First, I do not believe that Aveline killed Lord Beckenham.'

'No?' Bognor watched a five-year-old in a sailor suit whirl an electric trimaran through a figure of eight.

'No,' said 'Q', and paused. 'You're too young to remember the Mitován affair?'

'If you say so.'

'I say so,' said 'Q'. 'Mitován was a Yugoslav. Wrong to call him Serb or Croat or anything else. He was before his time. Killed. Betrayed.'

'When?'

'Oh, during the war. The British parachuted him in. He had come out in 1938 with his younger brother.' 'Q' raised his stick and beat the ground three times hard. 'Bad business,' he said.

'And who betrayed him?'

'You can't guess?' Quizzical blue eyes peered into his, almost laughing, yet too compassionate for cheap laughter. 'We didn't know at the time, of course, and by the time we found out it was too late. In fact it was much neater to leave him in place.'

'The complexity of Intelligence operations never ceases to baffle me,' said Bognor sourly.

'Never ceases to baffle us all,' said 'Q'. 'Otherwise we'd all be a sight better at it, wouldn't you say?' He laughed again, an attractive punctuation mark. 'No,' he said. 'It's too serious to tease . . . Mitován was betrayed by the man who later became Lord Beckenham.'

'I see,' said Bognor.

'Your old friend Vole had got hold of it, of course. He came to see me a couple of times. That book of his would have been remarkable, though I doubt now whether it will ever see the light of day.' He paused and gazed ruminatively at the boats on the pond. 'There are certain things, I'm afraid,' and he spoke sadly now, 'which are better left unsaid. Offends a few principles one may hold, but can't be helped.'

Bognor prompted him gently. 'I have got the picture about Beckenham,' he said, 'but I don't think I fully understand where this business about the Yugoslav gets us.'

'Mitován,' said 'Q'. 'He was an attractive man, very. He'd have given Tito something to think about, but . . . well . . . the Germans put him in one of the camps. Doesn't bear thinking about, really. I don't believe he ever talked, despite what they did to him. . . .'

Bognor allowed the silence to drift for a moment and then said again, plaintively, 'Yes, but . . .'

'Mitován,' repeated 'Q'. 'Doesn't that mean anything? Ring no bells?'

'No,' said Bognor. 'I don't know any Yugoslavs.'

'You do in a manner of speaking. Remember I said he had a young brother he brought out of the Balkans with him? All the rest of the family had been massacred.'

'Yes, but I still don't see . . .'

'Perhaps,' said 'Q', 'my pronunciation is misleading. Jo was always keen to stress that last syllable, but when his brother changed the name he put all the emphasis up front.'

'Mítovan,' said Bognor. 'You don't mean . . . ?'

'That's exactly who I mean,' said 'Q'. 'I know what you're thinking, but it often affects people like that. He is a little more English than the English, but that's not uncommon. It takes foreigners like Daninos and Mikes to really caricature the English. We're not nearly so extreme.'

'And you think he avenged his brother?'

'In fact I know,' said 'Q', very seriously now. 'But listen to me.' He bent his head low and spoke very softly to the younger man. 'The slate is clean. It was the only honourable course. It's right that you should know. How right it is for others to know I'm not certain. That's for you to decide. It's your case. Yours and Dr Frinton's. I'm sure you'll make the right decision.'

He stood. 'Goodbye then,' he said. 'I don't suppose we shall meet again. And by the way, don't be too hard on poor Parkinson. He does his best.' And with a trace of a smile, more evident in the eyes than around the mouth, 'Q' waved his cane, turned and vanished among the nannies and their charges.

Bognor sat on the bench for a moment, then ran to the park gates and hailed a taxi for Paddington Station.

He reached Apocrypha Great Gate shortly after two, and hurried at once to Mitten's rooms. They were empty. He then walked briskly across the quad to Dr Frinton's rooms. There was no one there either. He had not banked on this. The revelations of 'Q' were too sensitive and explosive to be entrusted to the public telephone, and he had to make personal contact. Now the only two people to whom he needed to talk had disappeared. There was the chief-

inspector chappie, but against much of his training and
many of his inclinations he had decided that the inspector's
involvement was going to have to be prematurely curtailed.
This was one time when town was going to be rigorously
excluded by gown. It smacked of privilege, of the age-old
arrogance of Apocrypha, and Bognor was deeply unhappy
about it. On this sad occasion, however, he could think of no
alternative.

He walked back to the Lodge and asked the porter if Mr
Mitten was in college.

'Yes, sir.'

'But he's not in his rooms?'

'No, sir. He's in the Senior Common Room.'

'And Dr Frinton.'

'Yes, sir.'

'What? She's in the SCR too? In that case I'll pop along
and dig them out.'

'I wouldn't do that, sir.'

'Oh. Why not?' The porter seemed surprisingly serious.

Bognor frowned. He hoped there hadn't been any more
corpses since he left town.

'It's a college meeting.'

'That's all right. They're probably only talking about
drains. They'll be glad to be hauled out.'

'Not drains they're talking about this time, sir.' He bent
down to the small hole in the glass between them. 'It's the
mastership,' he said *sotto voce*. 'I believe they're electing Lord
Beckenham's successor.'

Bognor swore. This was indecent haste. Beckenham
hardly cold, and already they were electing someone to take
his place. On the other hand, the rumour and speculation
and scandal were so rife that speed might seem essential to
some Fellows. He tried to think straight. If they were carrying out an election this early, there would have been no time
to wheel out the host of impressive outside candidates from
Whitehall, Westminster and the BBC who usually jostled for
jobs like this. They could only be meeting to elect an internal
candidate, and the most obvious internal candidate by far
was Mitten himself. In fact you might say it was the merest of
formalities. 'Oh, bloody hell!' he said and swung

round and ran off towards the Senior Common Room.

The Apocrypha SCR was actually a complex of rooms, the first of which was a straightforward entrance hall. The door was locked and it was opened after repeated knocking by the formidable figure of Bell, the College butler, who allowed him into the hall but no further.

'This is vital,' snapped Bognor, who had never liked Bell even when he was a relatively junior scout during his own undergraduate days. 'It is a matter of life and death, not to mention the good name of the College.'

The good name of the College meant much more to Bell than life and death, but he was not to be swayed. He remembered Bognor as well as Bognor remembered him, and with no more enthusiasm. It was clear to both men that this was what contemporary jargon would call an irresistible force—immovable object situation. Bognor realized that he had no more chance of getting into the election meeting than he would have had of making it into the Sistine Chapel when the cardinals were choosing a pope. 'If,' he suggested, 'I give you a note for Dr Frinton, will you deliver it?'

Bell seemed to consider this for an age, but eventually he said he supposed there was no harm in it.

Hastily Bognor ripped a page from his diary and scribbled the message: 'Mitten dunnit. Total gen. Am outside. Com quick. Bognor, Board of Trade.'

He supposed Bell would read it, but that was too bad. With any luck he wouldn't understand it. The next few minutes passed excruciatingly slowly. Bognor paced and tried to collect his thoughts, but they were hopelessly and irretrievably confused. At last the note worked, and Bell came out with Hermione in tow. She was wearing haute couture jeans, her MA gown and an expression of extreme irritation. Bognor thought she had never looked lovelier.

'Darling,' she said, waving his note at him. 'What is all this rot? It had better be good. We're just about to vote.'

Bognor closed his eyes. 'You must not vote. You must absolutely not vote. It would be a disaster for the College.'

'I can't agree,' she said. 'Best to get it out of the way. Waldy will make a perfectly adequate Master and we can't stand any more two-ring circuses at the moment.'

'But you can't elect a man who has just murdered his predecessor,' hissed Bognor. 'It'll be like the Wars of the Roses.'

'I think you had better explain,' said Dr Frinton in a voice that would have doused the fires of hell.

Bognor did, rapidly, skidding round corners, taking the facts at reckless speed, but wrapping the whole story up in not much more than five minutes flat.

'You mean Waldegrave is a Yugoslav?' she said. 'But that's preposterous. He's no more Yugoslav than you or I. If he's a Yugoslav then I'm a virgin.'

'It's true.'

'You're off your rocker, darling.'

'You can be a very obstinate and silly woman,' he said. 'There is more to life than *Beowulf* and Bolislav.' He tore another page from his diary. 'If *you* won't believe me, maybe *he* will.' And he scribbled another note. 'I know everything,' it said. 'Please come out now. Bognor.' He folded it up and wrote on the outside, 'Mr Mitován.'

The next few minutes of pacing seemed even longer than the last, but at length the door to the electoral chamber was opened and Waldegrave Mitten came out on his own. He was looking, appropriately yet paradoxically, extraordinarily English in his shabby tweed jacket and canary-coloured cardigan. Bognor saw at once that his hands, at least metaphorically speaking, were up.

'I'm sorry,' said Bognor.

'I can't say I am,' said Mitten. 'It was too good for him, going like that.'

'You can't be Master, I'm afraid.'

'To be honest, it's rather a relief.'

Mitten smiled and Bognor smiled back, one Apocrypha man to another.

Epilogue

'So you see,' said Bognor, squeezing lemon on to his smoked salmon, 'I've connived in a cover-up.'

His wife frowned. She had a stuffed leg of lamb *en croûte* in the oven, to go with the celebratory Château Cantemerle.

'Isn't it a bit of a risk?' she said. 'And well, without being puritanical about it, well, *wrong*?'

'He only killed him,' said Bognor.

'That's what I mean.'

'Aveline and Beckenham killed lots of people. Or had them killed.'

'And the poor chief-inspector chappie doesn't suspect anything?'

'I think he does suspect a little.' Bognor's eyes glazed as he contemplated the exquisite fish. 'But he knows he's outranked. National security is more important than common or garden justice.'

'I don't like the sound of that,' said Monica.

'No,' said Bognor. 'But there's justice and justice. *I* think it's been done, and if Aveline is credited with one extra piece of bloodiness, who cares except him? Besides, it's useful propaganda if the world believes that Soviet moles are given to knocking each other off when the going gets rough.'

'I suppose so,' said Monica. She seemed dubious.

'And I have also had a word with the right people about Edgware, Crutwell and Rook,' said Bognor with satisfaction. 'There's a spanner in their works all right.'

'And Mitten keeps his old job at Apocrypha?'

'Absolutely. They'll just have to find a new Master from

somewhere else.' Bognor chewed thoughtfully. 'They need a sound, reliable, decent old Apocrypha man of integrity, ability. . . .' He drank a little Gewürztraminer and rolled it round his mouth. 'Do you suppose,' he asked, 'that Parkinson would give me a decent reference?'

*On the following pages are details of Arrow
books that will be of interest.*

BLUE BLOOD WILL OUT

Tim Heald

Frederick, third Earl of Maidenhead, had woken at six-thirty, drunk one cup of tea from the Teasmade machine and put on a pair of individually styled bathing trunks with FM embroidered on the left leg. While the rest of Sir Canning's guests slept, he was drifting downstream. He appeared to be making no effort to swim further; his arms and legs were perfectly limp. He was, of course, extremely dead . . .

For Simon Bognor, the assignment had begun with a boiled egg and a call from the office. It had been a long and one-sided conversation, but more cheerful than he was used to. He had no way of knowing exactly how typically awful things would soon become. Or that, in a few days, he would have to admit that his opinion as to who the killer might be would include some of the bluest blood in the land. Of course, Simon would also agree that it was just as likely that the butler had done it.

£1.00

DEADLINE

Tim Heald

Shortly after eleven o'clock that evening, St John Derby, the editor of the Samuel Pepys column of the *Daily Globe*, had lurched himself into his office, poured himself a drink and rung the nightwatchman for a cab. When Albert came up to tell him that the taxi was downstairs, he found the reveller slumped across the blotter. He attempted to shake St John into motion. But St John Derby was not just drunk. He was, of course, extremely dead . . .

It was painfully obvious to all concerned that Bognor's talents, whatever they might be, were wasted in his job. The qualities demanded of men in the Department were patience, courage, ruthlessness and cunning. Simon Bognor was impatient and cowardly, squeamish and straightforward. He was poor at poker, and becoming increasingly set in his ways. What the hell was he doing on this case?

£1.00

JUST DESSERTS

Tim Heald

Escoffier Savarin Smith was sitting at a table in the kitchen of his celebrated restaurant, white linen napkin tucked into his shirt front, having his customary pick-me-up after everyone had gone. In front of him were two full bottles of Krug, a great deal more than usual. When work began after breakfast, *le patron* was found sprawled forward across the table, head resting between the empty bottles. He was, of course, extremely dead . . .

Simon Bognor of the Special Investigations Department was a man ill-equipped by nature, upbringing and experience for the painstaking and sensitive job in which he found himself. Like others doomed to work which was beyond them, he took some solace in food and drink. It was this one small claim to being a gourmet that caused his being assigned to the Smith case – which was almost enough to turn even Bognor against food forever.

£1.10

THE SCENT OF FEAR

Margaret Yorke

Mrs Anderson was afraid that she was losing her mind. She was beginning to forget where she had put things, what she had bought, even what she had eaten. Living all alone in the rambling mansion that had been her home for fifty years, Mrs Anderson was isolated from the town, forgotten by her relatives, and had outlived all her friends.

But Mrs Anderson was not quite alone. She had a visitor. A young man who came every night, through the dining room window. Who helped himself to food and money, who had even made a comfortable room for himself in the attic. A young man who enjoyed power. He could take over the house and make it his kingdom whenever he chose – whenever he needed a place where no one would ever think of looking for him, where no one would find him, no matter what he'd done . . .

'With every novel Mrs Yorke has become more assured' *Daily Telegraph*

'Tense, well written . . . you'll read every word' *Current Crime*

£1.25

THE COST OF SILENCE

Margaret Yorke

The body lay sprawled, the face contused and battered, the skull crushed . . .

Emma Widnes might have died at any moment, or she could have lived for years. Her husband, Norman, was certainly the kindest nurse his incurable wife could wish for. But then Norman was so pleasant to everyone – a blameless shop-keeper in a quiet town.

The murdered body of Emma Widnes shocked the most experienced of CID detectives, and soon Bidbury reverberated with whispers and conjecture.

And the skeletons could be heard, rattling in the most unlikely cupboards . . .

'Intrigue and deception with a delightfully unexpected twist as a final page bonus' *Financial Times*

'A compelling read' *Irish Times*

£1.25

Ruth Rendell

'Britain's new Queen of Crime' *Daily Mirror*

Ruth Rendell is one of Britain's top crime novelists, and her books are available from Arrow. You can get them from your local bookshop or newsagent, or you can order them direct. Just tick the titles you require and complete the form below.

☐	THE BEST MAN TO DIE	£1.25
☐	A DEMON IN MY VIEW	£1.50
☐	FROM DOON WITH DEATH	£1.50
☐	THE FACE OF TRESPASS	90p
☐	A GUILTY THING SURPRISED	£1.25
☐	A JUDGEMENT IN STONE	£1.50
☐	THE LAKE OF DARKNESS	£1.50
☐	MAKE DEATH LOVE ME	£1.25
☐	MASTER OF THE MOOR	£1.50
☐	MURDER BEING ONCE DONE	£1.25
☐	A NEW LEASE OF DEATH	£1.25
☐	PUT ON BY CUNNING	£1.25
☐	SHAKE HANDS FOREVER	£1.25
☐	A SLEEPING LIFE	85p
☐	SOME LIE AND SOME DIE	90p
☐	TO FEAR A PAINTED DEVIL	£1.50
☐	WOLF TO THE SLAUGHTER	£1.25

Postage _____

Total _____

ARROW BOOKS, BOOKSERVICE BY POST, PO BOX 29, DOUGLAS, ISLE OF MAN, BRITISH ISLES

Please enclose a cheque or postal order made out to Arrow Books Limited for the amount due including 10p per book for postage and packing for orders within the UK and 12p for overseas orders.

Please print clearly

NAME ....

ADDRESS ....

....

Whilst every effort is made to keep prices down and to keep popular books in print, Arrow Books cannot guarantee that prices will be the same as those advertised here or that the books will be available.